Young W

what's the story?

CENTRAL SOUTHERN ENGLAND

Edited by Annabel Cook

First published in Great Britain in 2003 by
YOUNG WRITERS
Remus House,
Coltsfoot Drive,
Peterborough, PE2 9JX
Telephone (01733) 890066

SB ISBN 1 84460 304 0

FOREWORD

This year, Young Writers proudly presents a showcase of the best short stories and creative writing from today's up-and-coming writers.

We set the challenge of writing for one of our four themes - 'General Short Stories', 'Ghost Stories', 'Tales With A Twist' and 'A Day In The Life Of . . .'. The effort and imagination expressed by each individual writer was more than impressive and made selecting entries an enjoyable, yet demanding, task.

What's The Story? Central Southern England is a collection that we feel you are sure to enjoy - featuring the very best young authors of the future. Their hard work and enthusiasm clearly shines within these pages, highlighting the achievement each story represents.

We hope you are as pleased with the final selection as we are and that you will continue to enjoy this special collection for many years to come.

CONTENTS

Jonathan Aldridge	70
Robbie Treadwell	71
Georgina Moore	72
Dean Brown	73
Kelsey Green	74
Stephanie Jones	75
Curtis Jefferies	76
Andrew Dao	77
Katie Gillett	78
Joseph Wilcox	79
Sian Flanagan	80
Olivia Rogers	81
Rebecca Johnson	82
Emma Hunter	83
Rosina Jacobs	84
Lucy Gorst	85
Dominic Grace	86
Lauren Clarke	88
Rebecca Fish	89
Louise Churchill	90
Ciara Gill	91
Nathan Simpson	92
Adam Walker	93
Paige Benham	94
David Gower	96
Olivia Shillabeer	97
Elizabeth Brewer	98
Maisie Dunning	99
Candie Glascodine	100
Alexandra Wigmore	101
Matthew Walker	102
Shannon Hamerston	103
Rachel Hunt	104
Matthew Hall	105
Lauren Sansom	106
Danielle-Elyse Fordham	107
Louise Goral	108
Wesley Jameson	109

Luke Jackson	110
Andrew Sheppard	111
Lydia Gyngell	112
Philip Baker	113
Emily Curtis-Bennett	114
Gareth Jenkins	115
Patrick Roberts	116
Zachary Bryan	117
Stuart Lane	118
Amy Rickman	119
Charles R Gilbey	120
Daniel Coe Vissenga	121
Elizabeth Heygate-Browne	122
Jack Walden	124

Holbury Junior School, Southampton

Emma Humphrey	125
Bethany Keen	126
Lauren Burrow	127
Chloe Smith	128
Kyla Armstrong	130
Shane Wynn	131
Sam Read	132
Ellisha Nemec	133
Hannah Duffy	134
Sarah Babey	135
Becky House	136
Sam Goodchild	137
Liam Smith	138
Todd Lloyd	139
Katie Knight	140
Richard Wells	141
Victoria Woolley	142
Dayle Andrews	143
Joshua McPhee	144
Tara Parry	145
Rhianon Jones	146
Jamie Hooper	147

Cadan Emsley 148
David Burn 149
Stuart Taylor 150
Kimberley Longman 151
Ashley Lewis 152
Abigail Pearson 153
Thomas Last 154
Abbie Mitchener 155
Lois Wheeler 156
Emily Heron 157
Elisha Dixon 158
Skye Wright 159
Michael Switzer 160
Suzanne Sayce 161
Grant Morgan 162
James McLaughlin 163
Nicola Duhig 164
Carmen Lever 165
Jade Perks 166
Daniel Lee & Brendan Jones 167

St Mary Star of the Sea Catholic Primary School, St Leonards-on-sea
Thomas Gillespie 168
Rachel Bone 169
Mark Longmire 170
William Calcott-James 171
Elliot Simmons 172
Charlotte Dowling 173
Ashleigh Humberstone 174
Rhian Jones 175
Osian Veall 176
Sarah Wainwright 177
Elinor Adie 178
Louis Friedlander 179
Robert Clifford 180
Diva-Lee Braine 181
Melodie Bright 182
Sam McShane 183

Daniel Gillespie	184
Jennifer Meredith	185
Bethany Groombridge	186
Ryan Byas	187
Jessica Martin	188
Kimberley Pain	189
Sofia Whitaker	190
William Oshuntoki	191
Lauren Henson	192
Andrew Russell	193
Jackson Mann	194
Ellie Thorne	195
Adaeze Chikwendu	196
Gabrielle Lacey	197
Melita Cameron-Wood	198
Alexander Byott	199
Kirsten Brightiff	200
Evie Clifford	201
Victoria Cordeux	202

Sharps Copse Primary School, West Leigh

Shannon Woolmer	203
Bradley Matthews	204
Darren Martin	205

West Blatchington Junior School, Hove

Liam Holdaway	206
Rhian Hart	207
Ayesha Begum	208
Amy Whelan	209
Lucy Bone	210
Shannon Brown	211
Megan Hogan	212
Sadia Atmani	213
Lilli Petrosian	214
Ellen Hodgkins	215

The Stories

ALFIE AND ALPHASMART

One day a huge rocket landed on Earth from space and out stepped a rather weird, but friendly-looking alien. He had one beady, twinkling little eye, a smiling moon-like face and a pointed, pink nose. He also had a pair of huge, silvery wings, two long, tube-shaped, metallic ears and two pairs of legs. He was called Alfie, the alien inventor. Alfie the alien had always wanted to visit the planet and meet the *humans!*

Alfie landed on a grassy meadow surrounded by trees. He could hear the earthly birds singing and the green leaves rustling on the trees. Though Alfie looked rather weird, he was the most gentle and caring alien that probably ever lived on the planet Jupiter. He looked around himself and said, 'Earth may not be so bad after all.' He then peered through his telescope - he could see strange-looking creatures walking down and talking to one another. Alfie whispered to himself, 'These must be the *humans.'*

As Alfie was watching through his telescope intently to see what was happening, he saw a little human girl with curly blonde hair sitting all by herself sobbing bitterly. Alfie flew up to the sobbing girl and sat beside her. 'Hello!' Alfie said to the little girl.
The girl laughed as soon as she saw Alfie and exclaimed, 'Are you an alien?'
Alfie replied, 'Yes, I'm Alfie, the friendly alien.'
The little girl said, 'I'm Alice and I'm crying because I'm lonely and I have too much homework to do.'
Alfie put his huge, silvery wings around Alice and hugged her tight.
Alice was taken aback and said, 'You are very sweet, thank you.'
Alfie told Alice, 'I'm going back to my rocket and I shall design a miniature robot friend for you who will also be able to help you with your homework.'

Alfie then went back to his lab in the space rocket and a little later, he had created a miniature, clever robot called Alphasmart. Alphasmart resembled a talking calculator with tiny, magical buttons, a rather large display screen, a beaming face and a pair of hands and feet.

Alfie the alien inventor handed Alphasmart proudly to Alice. He also said to her, 'Look after this intelligent chap, he will be your robot friend from now on.' Alfie then waved goodbye to Alice and flew off in his rocket, back to Jupiter.

Alphasmart travelled in Alice's school bag to and from school every day. Soon Alphasmart became a genius and could do lots of smart things like -
When he was one he could study bones
When he was two he could count to 500,000
When he was three he could swim in the sea
When he was four he was more of a computer whizz kid!
When he was five he had become a walking encyclopaedia and a mathematician.

Alphasmart soon became a big hit with all the kids in Alice's school. Alphasmart even taught the children how to keep the environment clean and green, and the importance of recycling. The children soon learnt from Alphasmart that they would have to show more love, caring, sharing and togetherness with one another. Alphasmart always had the correct answer to every question in the world, be it about science, history, geography, French or anything else. He could quickly solve any difficult problem, puzzle, riddle or brain teaser. He also explained to the children about space and the solar system and how important it was to love the other planets and its people. The children always enjoyed listening to and learning from Alphasmart.

On his sixth birthday, Alphasmart decided to return to Jupiter where he and his family belonged. So after waving a sad farewell to Alice and all the children in her school, Alphasmart set off in a special rocket back to Jupiter.

From that day onwards, Alice and her friends occasionally visited the grassy meadows and spent hours watching the countless, little, gleaming stars in the sky. They used to shout, 'Alfie and Alphasmart, we miss you and we will always love you!

We send all our love from Earth to everyone on Jupiter.'

Therefore, the next time when someone tells you, 'I met an alien the other day with one beady, twinkling little eye, a smiling moon-like face and a pointed nose', you bet it's Alfie from Jupiter checking on you!

Tanuvi Ethunandan (8)

THE RUBY NECKLACE

The mist curtained the sunrise, peeping up from behind the tops of the mountains. Trees were swaying slowly as a high wind picked up, whistling through the deserted countryside. Rabbits scampered hastily as a young girl - around the age of ten - skipped blissfully, like a butterfly when finding its flower, forgetting, for the moment, about her purpose. A necklace, which shone brightly, so brightly that it could blind the naked eye, was worn around her neck, underneath her cream blouse. Her feet came to a steady halt outside a dark, shadow-filled forest. The gnarled branches of the trees curled inwards and seemed to stare at her suspiciously. 'Hell-hello!' she spoke nervously, before taking a small step inside the unwelcoming habitat, to place the necklace in the heart of the forest, as she had been told by her mother.

Meanwhile, back in their thatched cottage, a few fields from where Dorothy found herself, an old lady lay upon a cobwebbed bed, barely breathing.

Sprinting back towards the entrance of the forest, Dorothy was finding it hard not to turn around to reclaim the necklace. It was that or her granny's death. 'I have no choice,' she murmured to herself, and continued running until she reached the scratched, old cottage door. In she ran, crying out loud, 'Gran, Granny.'
Was her granny alive? Slowly, the old lady's eyes opened and a smile was washed across Dorothy's face.
'Gran,' she whispered, 'oh, Gran.'

Eloisa Tovee (11)
Albourne CE Primary School, Hassocks

A Day In The Life Of Britney Spears

Last week I woke up and I was Britney Spears! I looked around the room, I saw golden chairs and I was sitting in a tremendously huge bed with a silver lining! I looked down, I had long, blonde hair, my skin was soft. I could not believe that I was really Britney Spears.

I opened my mouth to sing but nothing happened, not one sound, nothing.
Suddenly a plump old woman popped her head around the door. 'Come on Miss Spears you have a concert tonight.'
'What?' I tried to say again but nothing.
'Pop stars are so rude,' the old woman started muttering down the hall.

Later that day the servants figured it out and started giving me remedies like honey, vinegar, lemon juice and throat mixture and salt water but none of them worked. When I got to the concert my voice wasn't any better. If anything it had got worse. As I emerged onto the stage the hall became silent. I opened my mouth to sing but nothing happened. The hall erupted with anger, my worst fear had come true. People booed me but I kept on trying. One last time I thought, so I opened my mouth and at last I could sing!

In the end everything went well. After the concert I had a little snap at my servants. Then I went home, lay on my bed and took a long nap.

Chloe Burch (9)
Arundel Court Junior School, Landport

A Day In The Life Of A Monk

It was great! I woke up as a monk. I staggered up to my room but it wasn't my room anymore. It was an attic.

I had already put on the radio. I heard that the *Vikings* were coming. That night when I went to sleep all I could hear was crashing thunderstorms. I looked in the mirror. I had a bald patch on the top of my head and I wore a sort of dress with a little rope tied around it. My shoes were tattered.

I heard that great dragon faces which were carved were seen all around Northern Ireland. It could have only led to one thing - Vikings had come to raid Northern Ireland.

The Vikings were great warriors with hard helmets with big, pointy horns on either side. They wore tough netting stockings and big coats which were very protective so if anyone tried to hurt them they would be protected by the coats. They also owned a boat which was about 18 metres long. It had big, spiral shields on the left-hand side. It also had a big, scary and devastating dragon face on the prow.

People were bombarded and driven out naked or killed. Believe me it wasn't a pretty sight, I was there. The Vikings had took a lot from the monks who were very poor. The Vikings on the other hand were very rich and they just wanted to be greedy. They raided a lot of countries and towns.

Suddenly I was back at home. I had had a wonderful time. I would never forget it.

Leanne Murphy (8)
Arundel Court Junior School, Landport

A DAY IN THE LIFE OF AN ASTRONAUT

One day when I woke up, I found a spaceship in my garden. It was really, really big and I went to see what was inside. I knew that I should get out but it was too late, the door was already closed. I pressed lots of buttons. I pressed a red one to make the door open.

Suddenly, the spaceship blasted off like a shooting star and I was really frightened. I tried to call for help but nobody heard me. I landed on the moon and got out of the spaceship. There was a man on the moon.
'Hello,' I said, 'are you stuck on the moon?'
'Nooo! I'm the man on the moon, I live here.'
'Oooh.'
I got back into the spaceship and pressed a button. I flew off to Jupiter and saw sand. *Oops* I pressed another button and flew off to Pluto. It was really freezing cold. *Oops,* I kept on flying to dangerous planets. I kept on pressing millions and billions of buttons but nothing happened. Suddenly I flew off to Earth and saw lots of schools and I was late for my writing competition.

When I got home my mum and I went into the spaceship and went to space. The spaceship was broken, but not all of it. It couldn't turn and was tumbling towards the sun. We needed some help.
'Help, help, somebody help!'
Nobody could hear us but they could see us.
'Look there's two people in a spaceship stuck there.'

The astronauts hooked a rope onto our spaceship and we climbed onto the rope to the astronauts' spaceship. Our ship blew up. We went back home for a nice supper.

Shamim Ahmed (8)
Arundel Court Junior School, Landport

WHERE DID THEY GO?

I was at my best friend's sleepover. Mattie is her name. She is so funny, kind and caring. I would not know what to do if she was not there. I mean that.

At around midnight, we started to tell ghost stories. Alice was the best, so we left her till last.

When Alice's turn came around, everyone got excited. We snuggled in together as we all knew we would be spooked. I closed my eyes to get the real feeling.

'One night,' she began, 'a cold, frosty night, a wooden, rotten house sat upon Dark Mount Hill. There was a rumour that the house was haunted. A young, foolish boy decided to prove everyone wrong. So on that night he headed to Dark Mount Hill. He jumped over the broken brick wall and landed on the solid mud floor. The house looked even spookier closer, but he shrugged off what his subconscious thought. He took one step, then another until he reached the house. He was certain he saw someone, but not a solid person. Anyway he pushed the door. There was a gush of ice-cold wind as he entered. His soul went with the wind. That boy was never seen again.'

A shiver ran down my spine. I opened my eyes but no one was there. I was alone, where did they go . . . ?

Nicole Hookey (10)
Arundel Court Junior School, Landport

SHADOW

One thundery, dark night, Steve was walking back from school. His house was at the other side of the woods. He was walking back from school when it was dark because he'd had computer club straight after karate. When he walked back he heard the owls hooting and he was shivering because he'd forgotten to take his coat with him. But today was different - he saw a castle that he'd never seen before.

Now it was getting late, so he thought he would go in to see if anyone was in there. As he pushed the wooden door open he knew it was a haunted castle. The floor was damp and the air had a musty smell. As he walked up the stairs he could smell mould. Suddenly he saw a shadow. He was definitely feeling scared and started to shiver.

When he was nearly at the top of the stairs the floor started to creak. Suddenly he saw the shadow again. There were some candles in some of the corridors. He could see cobwebs with no spiders. The candles went out and he saw gleaming eyes. Then he heard crashing and thunder from outside. There was silence, then *footsteps*. Then he started to get terrified.

He followed the shadow. It went into a room, he followed it. He closed the door behind him. He got freaked out and decided to go back out, but he *couldn't!*

Connor Mayes (10)
Arundel Court Junior School, Landport

I WISH I WAS AN OLDEN DAYS TEACHER

One busy day in the countryside everyone was rushing around and I was reading a book about an olden days teacher, it was very scary. I really wished I was one of those teachers so I could hit people with a cane if they talked, were silly or didn't listen to what I said, although sometimes I'd be nice and share my sweets from the sweet jar I made.

In our school the teachers were not mean at all. They didn't hit you or put you in for the whole day like the mean teachers. They even let you have extra play. Every time we got to play I was always a teacher, but I didn't hit people. I only pretended to hit them. I was always very kind. Whenever we had to be something in a lesson I wanted to be a teacher.

Days passed on but the same things were happening as I grew and grew. I was nearly a teenager and I was pretending to be an olden days teacher. A few more days went past, then I was a teenager. More days went past, then I was an adult. I could still remember that I wanted to be a teacher because I wrote in my diary.

My dad said, 'If you want to be a teacher, you have to be one, learn loads of things, like be nasty.'

When I was 25 I was a teacher, a good teacher.

Abida Khatun (8)
Arundel Court Junior School, Landport

THE HAUNTED HOUSE

'Just another ordinary day, always rain, rain, rain,' Tom sighed.
'You just have to live with it sometimes love,' said Tom's mum,
Caroline, in a sweet voice.
Crash!
'What on earth was that?' they shouted. Tom and Caroline ran up the
stairs. There was nobody there.
Ding-dong!
Tom's mum opened the door. 'Tom, will you come down.'
'Sure Mum, I'm coming.' When Tom came down, his mum told him to
follow her.

Tom was in the living room. 'Dad! Dad, who's she?'
'Her, that's your cousin Lucy,' Nick replied. 'Lucy, why don't you go
with Tom, you can see if anybody's upstairs.'
'OK then.'
When Tom and Lucy were looking, Lucy was telling Tom about a story
she had heard. It was about a girl who lived in a haunted house.

One day she went upstairs because she heard something, so she started
to investigate. She went up the stairs and walked into a room. The girl
walked further into it. She felt a cold hand touch her shoulder. She was
never seen again.

Bang!
'What was that Lucy?' Tom cried, in a worried voice.
Lucy wasn't there.
'Lucy, where are you? Lucy?'
All of a sudden, Tom felt a shaky hand clench his arm . . . *whoosh.* In
seconds, Tom had vanished. Lucy, with an evil grin on her face, was
feeling very pleased with herself.

Ameenah Begum (8)
Arundel Court Junior School, Landport

THE MURDER GAME

Jon had never run this fast. His heart was pounding fiercely in his chest and although he knew stopping for a second would be OK, there was something sinister in the way the figure was so casually walking after him, so he continued to run.

He was sprinting blindly now, which was unfortunate. He did not see the barbed wire fence, nor did he see the root that sent him toppling onto it.

The body was found the next day. It appeared that Jon Whitman had been taking a late stroll, when he tripped and his neck became entangled in the fence. There were no signs of murder though. The killer was careful.

It cackled psychotically to itself in its abandoned warehouse home. That was the fourth 'accidental' death brought upon Rednie Hill and the next kill was already planned.

It was late and Emily was driving home when she saw the man. He was signalling for her to pull over. Reluctantly, she eased her car to a halt. Then she saw the knife. Terrified, she forced her car forward. The man just stood helplessly by a tree as the car screamed towards him.

The police came and promised to lock him up for years. If only they'd got the real man, not a man who'd stolen the killer's knife so that when he'd warned Emily she'd have believed him. So the killer was still free, plotting revenge on the man that had nearly ruined it all.

Joe Butler (11)
Burwash CE Primary School, Etchingham

HECTIC DAYS

Her luxurious bed lounged around her as the purple alarm clock on Jessie's bedside table rang. It was nine-thirty and she had to be at work by eleven. She slowly emerged from her nest, walked over to the kitchen and made some breakfast.

When Jessie was dressed, she had to make a move. Her partner drove her up to Walford Street and then said goodbye. He said he'd pick her up by eight. Jessie watched him drive off, then went to where the other actors were.

Although Jessie was tired, her acting was great. The day went very slowly; Jessie was nearly worn out. Despite her being bored, Jessie still adored performing.

Work eventually finished and Jessie went to get something to eat. She stood waiting for her partner's Jaguar to turn up. Soon enough it came and Jessie was taken home.

When finally she got back, Jessie and her partner walked into the kitchen. It was good to be home she said to herself as she shoved her bag on the side.

After bathing, Jessie decided to go to bed. She wanted to lie there forever. However, she had to be up early in the morning. She felt her eyes shut tight and soon she was fast asleep. Jessie hoped she'd have a good night: tomorrow she had to become Kat Slater once again!

Jessica Shale (11)
Burwash CE Primary School, Etchingham

LIFE WRECKER

This is a story about a girl. She was eleven and perilous. She had no idea that adventures could send you to the place of no return.

May (that was the girl's name) was sitting on her bed when she decided to go to her local woods. She ran down the stairs and out of the door as quick as lightning. When she finally reached the heart of the woods, she saw in the corner of her eye the most stunning cottage she had ever seen. There was ivy climbing up the Victorian walls, with beautiful flowers outside. 'Wow!' she whispered. She ran over to it and knocked on its small, circle-shaped door.

'Hello,' an old woman said quietly. She seemed frail and happy she had a visitor.
'Hi, I'm May,' she said, 'who are you?'
'Come in and have some cakes and a drink. I'll tell you inside.'
So in they went.

They sat talking for a while, until the woman brought the cakes out. May stuffed her face for about half an hour, still blabbering on. Suddenly, every voice in the house stopped. After a few minutes of silence there was a high-pitched, everlasting, ear-piercing scream, followed by a vicious laugh.

The next day May's parents discovered she was missing. Even though they were distraught, they were angry that she had gone without telling them. They sent out many search parties but nothing was found. May had not only ruined her own life but also both her parents' lives.

Leila Hill (11)
Burwash CE Primary School, Etchingham

A LESSON LEARNT

I looked around warily, not wanting to be caught, this was it; I was going to shoplift.

Uh-oh.
'Can I help you Miss?' The owner of the shop looked down at me, her face lined with curiosity.
'I-I was just looking. Honestly.' My face relaxed into a smile as I tried to look calmer.
'Hhmm.' She gave me the benefit of the doubt.

As soon as she went, I stuffed CDs into my bag. When that was done, I ran outside and slid down the wall, sweat trickling from my forehead. I was startled when I heard some rough grunts from up above me.
'We saws youse take dem CDs dinnwe?' A gang of punky teenagers sneered at me.
'So what if you did?' I challenged.
'We'll beat youse ups and robs youse.' They were spitting mad now.
'I don't want 'em anyway.' I said, offering the CDs to them. I was trying to be cool, but inside I was crumbling. Why had I done it? Why? I asked myself this over and over as the gang of teenagers snatched the stolen goods and ran off.

I took a deep breath and then walked through the door of the police station.
'Ah! I thought we'd be hearing from you! Come in, make yourself comfortable, then spill the beans!'
I sat down, then told them all about my shoplifting. When I'd finished, the constable told me my offence was serious, but I just got a warning. This time.

That's one thing I'll never do again.

Isabel Alderson Blench (10)
Burwash CE Primary School, Etchingham

WHO'S IN THERE

Matt and Emma were in their secret den in the woods waiting for the crack of dawn. They had heard unknown voices and sounds coming from the house that had not been heard before.

They walked towards the abandoned home of the pests, they looked for an unlocked entrance. While inside searching for life, Matt and Emma checked different rooms. They had reached a door that no one had been in. As Emma opened it a gush of wind swooped in through the window and passed through her dark brown hair, then leaving a breezy chill around.

They both made their way into the lonely cellar, where they found lots of scattered junk around the floor of the room. A dripping oil can was found left on a dusty worktop. Rats were running around in each corner, screeching at each other. The rodents scrambled towards them, nibbling at their feet. The rats started to jump at them, becoming fierce. Big rats with thick, long tails and sharp red eyes crowded around. Matt and Emma moved slowly backwards away from them when Matt fell . . .

Harley Taylor (11)
Burwash CE Primary School, Etchingham

THE RETURN OF THE WITCHES

It all started on the 29th March, 1994. I strolled into a wood and started enquiring around. I could feel a gust of wind hit my face and blow my hair rapidly. Suddenly, right in front of my eyes were two hideous and frightful witches. I heard them cry with laughter as they swooped down and grabbed me. We were gliding through the air like when I parachuted out of an aeroplane.

After a couple of minutes we were outside a cave. I walked through and I felt a shiver down my spine as I turned pale. I put my hand on the wall and ripped it off sharply; I had a little graze on the end of my finger. The witches grabbed me again and tugged me and tugged me, like I was the rope in the middle of a tug-of-war, except for they were both pulling on the same end.

They got me into a room where all the walls were grubby. I gazed at a pot for a couple of seconds; they had picked me up and shoved me into the scalding water. Then they started pouring salt and pepper on me. I guessed they were going to eat me. I started struggling. I slid out of the pot and dashed towards the door. I felt relieved and animated. Suddenly, coming down towards me was an axe . . . !

Megan Davies (11)
Burwash CE Primary School, Etchingham

A DAY IN THE LIFE OF ALAN TITCHMARSH

I pushed open the wooden door and gazed into my summer wonderland garden. I plodded over to the murky green pond; took a great big smell of my relaxing place. It smelt like aloe vera washing powder with a hint of lemon.

I strolled over to the sky-blue summer house (freshly painted) to collect the fish food. Just as I left the summer house I saw my cat (Potato) digging up my sunflower seedlings. 'Pots!' I bellowed, and in shock, Pots bolted off, leaving the sunflowers looking like a bulldozer had trampled over them. I tipped the food into the water. It disappeared instantly.

I peered over to the deck and thought aloud. 'Should I paint the deck blue today or tomorrow? Tomorrow!' Then as it was a nice day, I decided to plant another aloe plant by the gazebo to increase the aloe vera smell. I picked up my shovel and started to dig. When I had planted the plant I covered the bottom with soil and pebbles.

I went to the holly tree and saw Pots sitting under there looking tearful, so I picked him up and gave him a cuddle. I put him down and he ran to the conservatory doors to be fed so I fed him, brushed him down and also locked up the house for the night.

Nicola Palmer (11)
Burwash CE Primary School, Etchingham

TRACY BEAKER

Hi, my name is Tracy Beaker. My mum is a famous actress who lives in Hollywood. She left me in an institution. All the people in this place call it the Dumping Ground.

Two years ago, Mum and I lived in an Indian jungle. We were the best explorers in the country. But that all changed when a producer came to involve us in Jungle Mania Two. Mum got the part of the detective. Her new toyboy shipped me up to here.

In the Dumping Ground live the helpers who are not exciting, not one bit. then I have my friends; there's only two of them, their names are Dolly and Ben. Now I have friends and enemies but I hate talking about them. As I was saying, I don't share a room. My walls are blue with white and red hot air balloons.

It was Saturday. As usual we went to the beach. It was Nathan's turn to take us. Dolly was first in the sea. Nathan got tea ready and we got changed. Dolly had her armbands on and swam too far out. All of us shouted, 'Nathan do something!' in high-pitched voices.
'I would but I can't swim!' Nathan shrieked.
As normal, I was there to save the day; after just starting to eat. I swam towards her. The rocks dropped down. I got Dolly on my shoulders.

Finally I was on the shore. Nathan dried us up and then we had tea and went home.

Hannah South (10)
Burwash CE Primary School, Etchingham

GHOST STORY

One day my friends and me went for a walk just before dinner. We went in the woods, it was beautiful. Before our eyes we saw a house, it looked abandoned and spooky. We heard music playing so we went in and we heard the whistling of a song.

We went upstairs to turn the music off and when we turned the music off the whistling stopped. Then we heard footsteps and the door shut on us. It was a ghost because we could not see anybody, but Tom was outside. We knew he was hurt and he would die. We looked through the keyhole as we saw the blade swish down . . .

After the door opened we jumped over Tom and followed the whistling, it went on for a long time, but it was a big house. Then it stopped. It was a big room, it had a toilet. We had split up by then and I heard two more of my friends scream . . .

Now there was only Ned and me left. We heard the whistling again and it was clear that when he whistled he was going to kill Ned and me, so we decide to run through the woods.

Finally we were nearly home. We could see the house through the trees but Ned and me were home and it was dinner time.

Grant Bird (11)
Burwash CE Primary School, Etchingham

GHOST STORY

One day in the graveyard I was walking and saw a rotting castle so I went in with Ned, Tom and Max. We heard a song it was the 'Jeepers Creepers'. A door slammed.
'Let's go upstairs and find out what the noise is,' said Tom.

As we went along, Max disappeared out of nowhere.
'Look there's a werewolf!'
'Hi my name is Batty Boy,' said the werewolf, 'what is yours?'
'Hi, I'm Nick, he's Tom and he's Ned.'
'I would get out of here,' said the werewolf.

Although we could see, we fell down a hole leading to a tunnel. The tunnel was dark and I think I heard rats. Then I saw some tails not very far away.
'L-l-look it's Max, he's on the wall,' Ned said.
'Where?'
'Behind you.'
Joe fainted.
Although Joe fainted, we went to a different castle without him. This time we hoped to see wizards and witches and did not want to see the werewolf again.

As we went into the castle we saw Joe was a pig. Suddenly the pig turned into a wizard.
'Would you like a cup of tea and a talk?' said the wise wizard. 'Well, did you know the castle was haunted?'
'No. We must be off, see you later.'

Robert Swaine (10)
Burwash CE Primary School, Etchingham

THE ADVENTURES OF TOM AND RIKI

Two adventurous boys, Riki and Tom, were looking for something to do on a dark and spooky night.

Tom decided to ask his brother if he wanted to go to the abandoned mansion below. They were both very excited about it, so they shot up to the door and went outside.
'Would you like a cup of cocoa?' their mum said, but it was too late, they had already gone.

As they reached the bottom, 'We're here,' they said together, 'let's explore.'

So they ran to the mansion, *bang!* Tom went into a coffin, *creak!* It fell down. They shrieked in horror, their hearts beating fast.

It was a vampire ghost. 'Leave! Leave me in peace!'
They froze in horror. 'Run,' they both shouted, so they ran home and banged on the door. 'Mum, we promise never to leave you alone again,' they said.

From that day on they never left again.

Riki Wright (11)
Burwash CE Primary School, Etchingham

SHALLOW NICK

I had tickets to ride the Titanica, a huge cruise ship that you travel to America on. Once I got on board I saw flags perched over the front of the boat (probably the countries that we were going to). I caught my reflection in the water and thought to myself, *God I'm pretty.* I turned around to catch a glimpse of a woman with a perfect figure. She wasn't as beautiful as me but sometimes you have to settle. I scuttled over to her and said smoothly, 'Hello lady,' and made a romantic sign.
'Who are you?' she said.
'Call me Nick.'
'Oh please, I'm looking for a man with a tender touch and I don't think you could fulfil those needs.'
'That's a lie.'
'Well take me out to dinner and prove it.'
'Alright then. Seven o'clock at the Moonlight Beach Club.'
'OK.'

I only had an hour to get ready so I slapped on manly cologne and I was off. It was a beautiful night; I met her at the end of the ship. She was looking out into the horizon. I strolled up to her, trying not to act scared. I kissed her romantically and we walked off hand in hand. Not quite what I expected - but I can live with it.

Nick Child (11)
Burwash CE Primary School, Etchingham

A Day In The Life Of An Astronaut

I awoke with a start as the piercing sound of my alarm clock echoed around my head. It was a very important day because I was going up to the moon. I peeled back the covers and slowly got dressed. Yawning, I stepped into my bright red Mini and pulled out of my driveway.

As I parked up in NASA's car park I was practically tugged out of the door by a mob of angry engineers, saying things like, 'Late, late, I can't believe he's late!' or 'His first time to the moon as well.'

'Blast-off in five four, three, two, one . . .'
I was thrown back in my chair as the rocket fought the force of gravity. Tears became streams as I went higher into the atmosphere. Finally I reached space and once again I was able to relax. I peered out of the window and was dazed by the most beautiful sight I had ever seen.

Suddenly I was jogged out of my daze as the rocket lurched forward and shot towards the moon like a bullet. The shuttle spun wildly out of control, travelling more and more quickly as it went. Finally it took one last leap and hit the hard surface of the moon.

I staggered out of the ship, along with a large gush of smoke. I peered around at the crater-filled surface of the moon. It wasn't what I would call stunning, but it had a very magical feel about it.

For several hours I explored, but then it was time to go home, so I climbed back into the ship and started the endless journey back to Earth.

As I landed back on the Earth's surface, huge cheers and flashes of cameras greeted me. I was then carried back to my bright red Mini on top of the swarming crowd. When I lay in bed that night, I thought how much I had enjoyed my trip and I did not regret a single minute of it.

Kelly Hill (11)
Fairlight Primary School, Brighton

THE DAY WE MOVED

One Monday afternoon me, Mum, Dad and my sister, Laura, went to a shop to see what houses were for sale. Mum thought she'd found one that would be right for all of us, so Dad went into the shop and bought the house.

The next day we got ready to move and my sister phoned for a van to take the furniture to our new house. Then suddenly, the doorbell rang, it was the man who had come to fetch the furniture. Mum and Dad got all the furniture into the van.

Three hours later we were at the new house, we were settling in well until I heard a noise coming from the bedroom upstairs. I went to look, but I could not see anything, then I thought to myself and said, 'It's a ghost.' So I ran downstairs and shouted, 'This house has ghosts!'
'Calm down!' Dad replied.
'No, don't be silly,' they all went.

But the next morning I went to look in the room and I could not see or hear anything. 'It's gone,' I shouted.
'See, there is nothing to worry about,' said Laura looking very ambit.

Then there was no sign of it at all.

Rebecca Hammond (11)
Fairlight Primary School, Brighton

A FACE AT THE WINDOW

David walked down the empty street as the icy wind lashed at his face. He had no idea that this would be the most terrifying day of his life.

As David walked down the icy road he felt the pitter-patter of rain on his head. It got harder and harder, so he took shelter in an old, abandoned house which looked more like a mansion than a house!

He looked around, but there wasn't anything interesting, just a bunch of old paintings covered in cobwebs. He suddenly heard a loud creak. He wondered if someone else had also taken shelter from the rain. He was shaking, but he told himself not to be scared and went upstairs. I know what you are thinking, you're thinking, *what a wimp, he's scared to go upstairs*. Well, wouldn't you be, if you were eight years old?

Now back to the story. He went into a room which seemed to be a study because that is where he heard the creak. There was a chair in the middle of the room which seemed to have a young boy sitting in it! David nearly had a heart attack when the chair turned around. It was his dorky brother James with his fake Hallowe'en blood all over his face! David did not shout or moan or beat the living daylights out of him, though a) he is older than him and b) he was used to it by now. So he just walked home not saying a word.

It was 9.30pm so David's mum told him to go to bed. All he had been doing since 6.30pm was reading. Anyway, he got ready for bed and cleaned his teeth. He noticed he could see that creepy, abandoned house from his bedroom window. He stared at it and then laughed to himself thinking how silly he had been.

He fell asleep as soon as his head hit the pillow and slept till the morning. I did say that he slept until the morning, 1.32am in the morning that is! He woke up hot and sweaty from a bad dream. He listened. Silence had fallen throughout the house and it was pitch-black.

He put his slippers on, stood up and turned the lamp on. He looked at the creepy house and its boarded up windows. Then he made his way quietly downstairs, got a glass of water and went back upstairs. He went to his window once more and his glass of water fell to the ground. The boarded up windows were not boarded up. There was a skeleton-like face sitting behind it, staring out.

David screamed, but no one could hear him.

Becky Marchant (10)
Fairlight Primary School, Brighton

LAST WEEK ALIVE

Big blue drips of water were splashing on the rooftops of people's houses. Emma and Daisy were alone watching TV and their parents had gone on holiday for a week. Emma thought it would be good to stay at home alone, but Daisy thought something bad was going to happen. After Daisy had calmed down they both watched TV.

While they were watching TV a gust of wind passed the window and slammed it shut. Then the TV switched off and the door shut. Emma and Daisy were horrified by the noise that they could hear. Daisy hid behind the curtain while Emma opened the living room door. Emma had to use all her strength to open the door, but she couldn't.

There was an old clock sitting in the corner of the room. Emma and Daisy started to talk when a tap on the wall came, but the strange thing was it was happening when the clock ticked and it ticked for an hour after the clock had chimed.

The clock had stopped, the door creaked open. Emma and Daisy ran through the door as quick as they could and shut it behind them. Just as they were about to run up the stairs, they saw two ghosts sitting in chairs calling them. Daisy passed out and stayed on the floor all night while Emma slept on the couch with the door shut.

When they woke up they were really scared, so scared that they slept over at their friend's house that night, but never told them what had happened.

That night the ghosts visited the house that they were staying in. This time the noise was much louder and only Emma and Daisy heard it. They both saw the ghosts wrapped up in chains and white cloth. They called out, 'Ghosts!' They disappeared and Emma's friend came running down the stairs. Emma's friend told them to go back to their own house and not to come back. So Emma and Daisy went home and prayed the ghosts would go away, but that didn't work. The ghosts kept coming back.

This time there were more and more coming by the minute. All of a sudden there was a knock at the door. Emma and Daisy looked out the window and saw that no one was there, but they still opened the door to find that two ghosts with two knives had just been stabbed in the chest and both fell to the floor.

Three days later Emma and Daisy's parents came home from their holiday. When they walked into the living room and found writing on the wall in blood, saying, *You're not safe!*

Craig Thurmer (11)
Fairlight Primary School, Brighton

THE HAUNTED HOUSE

After school Tom and Shara went to the woods. When it was 6 o'clock they went back home, but they did not know the way. So they picked the way to go, but they landed near a house. It looked like somebody hadn't lived in it for quite a while. It had a swamp full of mud so Tom and Shara knocked on the door, but there was no reply. Then the door opened by itself.

Tom and Shara went into the house, it was damp, the floors and furniture were soaking wet.

Their mum was worried so she called the police and said, 'My kids are missing, I can't find them.'

When the children heard a creak above them, they rushed out of the house but then the door closed on them. Then Tom and Shara heard footsteps coming down the stairs, foot by foot. They found a baseball bat in a cabinet and quickly hit him, but they missed and smacked the bat onto the wall. Shara screamed, but then the police heard the scream and went to check it out. The police saw a man and they caught him and saved the kids. They went safely home, but their mum wasn't very happy.

Jack Swannack (10)
Fairlight Primary School, Brighton

A Day In The Life Of A Fireman

Alarm goes off and I get up at 7.30 and go straight to the bathroom to brush my teeth and do my hair. Then I go back to the bedroom and get dressed ready for work. Then say goodbye to my family and get in the car and leave.

Finally, I arrive at work and then I get a call telling me something has happened and where it has happened. Very calmly I get my uniform on and jump into the fire truck.

As I arrive I can feel the heat from the fire. Immediately I get the fire hose out.
The captain shouts, 'Find out if anyone is in the house.'
Quickly I run over to the owner of the house and ask if anyone is in there.
All panicky and worried she says, 'Yes, my baby is trapped behind the flames, I tried to get him but I couldn't.'

In an instant I, (the fireman) get my safety gear on and go into the house. As I enter the house all I can see is thick, black smoke. There the baby is, in its cot, crying behind a wall of flames. I quickly put out the flames covering the door and slowly climb down the ladder with the baby in my arms and everybody cheers and runs over to help me down the rest of the ladder.

Safely I put the baby into its mother's arms and they both go off in an ambulance. The rest of the crew by then have put the flames out. Back at the station it is time for home and I get into the car and head home to bed.

Steven Williams (11)
Fairlight Primary School, Brighton

THE UNREAL JOURNEY

The rain beat against the frozen window. Katie and her little sister Yazmin were suffering from boredom. Wouldn't you be bored if it's a rainy day and you have to stay at your gran's house? So there was nothing to do,

Katie and Yazmin saw that Gran was asleep. So they snuck out of the house as quiet as mice. They thought of going to the Shell shop on the seafront. As they walked on and on, it got colder and darker. Katie could see that a storm was coming. Yazmin got scared. Then suddenly, a massive gust of wind carried Katie and Yazmin into the sea.

There was a boat nearby and a boy helped them. He put them in the cabin and lit a heart-warming fire and gave them a dose of medicine and took care of them.

The next morning Katie was disturbed by a singing voice and woke up. She was startled to see the young boy singing with such a beautiful voice. Katie said to the boy, 'What is your name?'
He replied, 'My name is Rory, what is yours, my lady?'
She said, 'My name is Katie and that is my sister Yazmin.'

Rory said that they were too far off the coast to go back so they would have to travel round Scotland to get back to the Brighton seafront. Yazmin had a buzz of adrenaline and rushed around the boat. Katie helped Rory get the boat ready and set off for Brighton.

It was not long after they had reached Scotland when there was something strange, like no sound, as if there was not a soul in Scotland. Katie and Yazmin took some food from the market for their dinner while Rory got some water to drink on the beautiful ship.

Katie made a spectacular feast. Rory and Yazmin were delighted. A sea monster jumped out of the freezing cold water. He spat his fearsome venom into the boat trying to kill them all. The sea water was lapping over the edge of the glimmering boat. The monster was casting venom like a snake. Rory tackled the monster to the death.

He climbed back into the boat and travelled to Rottingdean and there they slept.

In the morning they travelled a little further until they got to Brighton. Then *bam!* Katie found herself on the ground and walked home to Gran.

Lucie Stenning (11)
Fairlight Primary School, Brighton

IN THE DARKNESS

'It's cold, it's dark and I want to go home!'

'Oh will you shut up Jess, I'm trying to get us out of here. Do you really think I want to be stuck in this sewers in the middle of the night?'

The hours seemed to be getting longer, the night to be getting colder and still Oliver and Jessica hadn't managed to climb out.

'Ollie, Oliver, is that you?'

'Huh, what did you say Jess?'

'Was that you moving in the sewage trying to scare me?'

'No, do you think you heard somebody?'

'Yes, I think someone is watching us. Ollie I'm really scared now, can we get out of here please?'

'Okay, okay, but I think we are going to have to walk through one of these tunnels. Which one did you hear the sound come from?'

'That one, I think.'

'Right, that leaves us with five more. OK. Eenie-meenie-miny-mo, catch a tiger by its toe, if it screams let it go, eenie-meenie-miny-mo. Right then, come on Jess let's go!'

They walked through the smelly, wet, creepy sewers for a long time until they came to the choice of two more tunnels.

'Which one Jess? I'm leaving it up to you.'

'That one then, I just have a gut feeling.'

'Right then, that one it is!'

And again they set off through the tunnels and soon it started to become a bit of a drag. The same boring atmosphere and oh don't forget the rats.

Then suddenly they could hear the footsteps getting closer and closer.

'Quickly, come on run, come on, come on!'

'I'm going as fast as I can.'

Then out of nowhere and unfortunately for Jess she slipped and fell into the dirty sewage water.

'Ooow!'

'What's up Jess?'

'I've hurt my ankle, I can't go on. Go on without me.'

'Oh don't be so stupid Jess, you're my sister, but sometimes I wish you weren't.'

'What did you say?'

'Nothing and anyway we're not in some adventure film.'

'Feels like it!'

'Oh well, maybe it does, but I'm not going on without you, now get on my back.'

So Jess got on Ollie's back, still in pain and Ollie half-running, half-hobbling went as fast as he could.

Then in the distance they could see a shimmer of light beaming down into the darkness. Ollie didn't care how heavy Jess was. He ran and ran and ran as fast as he could to get to the open hole. Then finally he got there. They were so excited, they were going home, they were really going home. But then Ollie shivered, he could feel something wasn't right. He turned round and saw a dark figure running towards them.

'Quickly,' shouted Ollie. 'Get up the hole quickly, quickly, hurry up!'

'I'm trying, I'm trying!'

At last Jess was up.

'Right Ollie, I'm ready.'

'OK, hold my arm and try and pull me up.'

'Ooh, you're too heavy, I can't pull you up. Use your legs to help you try and walk up the wall!'

'Right, OK, 1, 2, 3.'

Ollie was desperate, he could hear the thing breathing. He was trying so hard then, then . . . he woke up. He was sweating buckets, he couldn't believe it, his dream felt so real.

Then suddenly his door slammed and in the dark he saw . . .

Jacob Fairminer Bray (11)
Fairlight Primary School, Brighton

GHOST STORY

'Bye,' Meygan's mum said as she went outside into the boiling hot front garden.

'Bye Meygan,' her little brother Mark shouted at the same time.

Meygan shut the door and sat down and watched a comedy show in the living room. Mark lay in his bed playing PlayStation games. Meygan had long brown hair and brown eyes and was 12 years old. Mark had brown hair and blue eyes and was two years younger than his sister.

Brring, brring. Megan muted the TV with the remote control that was in her hand and picked up the phone. 'Hello,' she said. It was her mum. 'I've got to remind you that I don't want you to go into the attic.'

'OK,' Meygan said.

'Why?' Meygan's mum answered.

'Because it's just dangerous up there. Bye-bye,' Meygan replied and put the phone down. She shouted up to Mark and said, 'Mum said don't go into the attic.'

'OK,' said Mark, 'I won't.'

Bang, bang. Meygan ran up the stairs to see what was going on. But no one was there apart from Mark. He was just sitting there playing his PlayStation. Meygan knew it wasn't him because he was playing the PlayStation. So they both got up and listened in to see what room it was coming from, it was the attic. Not remembering what their mum said they went up into the pitch-black room . . . they both grabbed a torch each. Standing there was a white see-through face and a white see-through body sitting down against an old box full of their old baby toys.

'Nan,' cried Mark.

'Shhh,' replied Megan. She walked over to the ghost. The ghost smiled at Meygan who was still walking closer and closer and then stopped.

'Hello,' Meygan said.

'Hello,' their nan said back.

'It's Nanny Wood,' said Mark. 'Come out of the attic,' said Mark. Then the ghost suddenly floated off into the front room, they followed close behind.

They asked her if she was lost and if she wanted to stay. She said yes.

Just then the doorbell rang. It was their mum, they quickly hid their nan back up in the attic and let their mum in.

Soon after that a couple of years passed and she is still living in that house.

Stevie Lee Healey (11)
Fairlight Primary School, Brighton

THE CAVE IN THE WOODS

One misty morning, Collin and Sophia were out walking in the woods, when they came to a nearby cave. Collin reached in to see if it was safe. Then they went inside to inspect the place. Suddenly a shattering of stones blocked the outside. Collin and Sophia could not go back, then a tiny, small, black spider came wandering around the small wet cave. They both followed the spider to a wide, cold, clean waterfall. Collin and Sophia saw a fat old man sitting on a stone on top of the waterfall.

The cave was full of bats and rats. The smell was awful and the cave was freezing. Nearby the fat man was a giant wise owl. The owl had red eyes and blue fur. The owl swooped towards the black spider and gobbled the spider up. The owl looked up. Its eyes were soon gleaming with fear. Collin decided to speak to the owl but there came no reply. Suddenly the bird grabbed Collin's ear and tried to bite it off, then Sophia jumped on its back and grabbed his arm. Soon the owl flew down to safety and Collin and Sophia looked at each other.
'Hello,' said the man with a cheeky grin, 'would you like to follow me?' Then he threw them into a cupboard with all the other children he had captured . . .

Christy Bean (11)
Fairlight Primary School, Brighton

STRUCK UNLUCKY

Thursday 12th

I was having an evening stroll down the park. I had just reached the swings when I saw the most unusual sight; a wolf riding the slide. Was I dreaming? I slapped myself hard and fell off the swing (it hurt). By the time I'd got up the wolf had gone. *I was dreaming,* I told myself. Walking home I saw my friend, Lisa.
'Hi Lisa,' I shouted.
'Yo Jo!' she answered.
'For the last time, my name is not Jo.'
'OK, it just rhymes.'
I got home, it was 11pm. 'I had better get to bed,' I said to myself.

I put on my pyjamas and got into bed. I lay in bed awake for ages. Somehow I didn't think the werewolf was a dream.

Friday 13th

'Yawn!' I had a huge yawn and went for my stroll. This time it was in the morning, but as I was swinging I was bitten. I don't exactly know what bit me, I only know it hurt. I turned round to have a look, I screamed and ran home. By the evening I was shuffling round my room in a weird fashion, sniffing at everything that I did not recognise.

That night I sat on my window sill and howled at the moon. Before I went to bed I ran away with the others calling me.
I called, *'Help me I'm a werewolf!'*
After, I ran into the night howling into the mist.

Emily Brown (11)
Greatham Primary School, Liss

HAUNTED

I was walking down the road when I did it. Adam crept up behind me and shouted, *'Boo!'* Unluckily I was already in a bad mood so I shoved him and he staggered out in front of a lorry. The brakes screeched as blood splattered everywhere. All I could do was run. I ran until I could go no further.

I looked around and found myself in some housing estate. This was where Adam's house was! And, sure enough, there he was up in his room. Then I realised Adam was lying, probably dead, on the road by the school. I screamed and the next thing I remembered was lying on my bed.

That night was terrible. I had nightmares about screeching brakes and pale, lifeless bodies. In the morning I was pale and clammy. At school Richard asked me where Adam was. 'Er . . . I think he's ill,' I replied. I looked down and saw a ghostly head in a pool of blood. After that, whenever I passed the point where I'd pushed him, I heard his blood-curdling scream.

One day it grew too much for me and I dived out in front of a lorry.

Tom le Vay (10)
Greatham Primary School, Liss

HORROR HOUSE

'Go on, I dare you!' challenged Steff.
'No,' Adrian knew entering House on the Hill meant never returning.
'Oh, come on you chicken, buck bwoark!'
'Okay, but you come too!'
'Fine,' shrugged Steff. 'I wanted to anyway.'

So the two began trekking up the hill towards the forbidden house, in the dusk, not knowing of the dangers that faced them.

The door slowly creaked open of its own accord as Steff walked up to it.
'Cool, just like being in the movies!' she exclaimed, walking in, Adrian following behind.

The dark hall was too much for the friends. They bolted towards the open door, but before they reached it, it slammed shut.
'Help!' cried Steff, beating at the door with her fists.
'Calm down,' soothed Adrian, taking charge, 'We'll just have to find another way out, like a back door.'
So they crept round, peeking into doors, but to no avail. On the last door they crept silently in. The door locked behind them.
'Arrrm!' whimpered Steff, tugging Adrian's sleeve.
'What?' Adrian snapped, turning round.
There, growing out of fungi patches on the floor, were disgusting, deformed zombies.

The two adopted a fighting stance. Adrian judo-flipped one zombie, as Steff punched another's chest. Suddenly, she felt a key in her hand. She thrust it in the lock, which clicked open. They ran flat out along the hallway, towards the open front door. They leapt through and zoomed down the hill to home.

Nick Evan-Cook (11)
Greatham Primary School, Liss

THE POLICE CHASE

It was early spring of 3000, when an alarm sounded at the National Westminster Bank in London. The bank had been broken into. The thief stole £20,000,000.

When police and detectives reached the bank the thief had gone and two men had been shot dead. 'This is not just a murder case, it's a robbery case too!' said Detective Meade.

In the police station detectives worked out that the thief had stolen a Ferrari car and was heading for the Bank of England. Twenty police cars and five FBI cars were speeding out of ten police stations in London. After half an hour all police and FBI had caught up with the suspect. After quarter of an hour three police had crashed and it was down to the twenty-two cars still on the road.

At approximately 12.30pm a huge lorry was driving through a crossroad. The Ferrari swerved to miss the lorry but ran someone over. The Ferrari crashed into a car and span around and hit three police cars and one FBI car.

The Ferrari was stopped by a lamp post. Then the suspect got out of his car, picked up his sack and ran on foot.

A police helicopter was then sent out! When the helicopter caught up with the suspect they started firing guns. Then police came in with bullet-proof jackets on. One hour later the suspect was shot in the leg. The chase was over! The thief was jailed for life and the money was returned.

Kyle Meade (11)
Greatham Primary School, Liss

TAKEN APART ALIVE

Dear Diary,

Let me take you back a year ago, it was Tuesday the 10th of October and I set off on a journey to the TAA house. I'd never been there before, I didn't even know what TAA stood for until now, but that will come up later in the story. Once I got there I was getting second thoughts, the house was old, creepy and looked haunted. I walked into the house but there was no one there.

I'd now spent a night at the house and everything had been OK, except for my imagination, however, on the third night, Friday the 13th, something strange was happening. There were voices, creaks and shadows. I got out of bed and looked around, an eerie creak sounded behind me, I spun around as quick as I could, nothing there. I got back into bed telling myself - *I'll leave tomorrow.*

After that I saw a shadow straight in front of me coming closer, and then with its hands it grabbed me round the neck, strangling me, it picked me up by the legs, carried me downstairs. Then . . . then he got my nose and took my brains out with a hook, through my own nose! He slit a slit on my body and took out my internal organs one by one. And now here I am as a spirit in the corner thinking, *next . . . next . . . it's my turn to kill! In the Taken Apart Alive house.*

Sammi-Jade Lowe (11)
Greatham Primary School, Liss

A SCHOOL PROJECT GOES WRONG!

Marco started walking home from school so that he could do his homework. He had to make a farm. His idea was a worm farm. He stepped into the door and his mum greeted him.

'Hello dear,' said Marco's mum, 'good day at school?'

'Not bad,' replied Marco.

He went straight into the garden to find a worm. He was digging for ages before he found one. Marco gently picked it up and went into his room. He made a pot full of dirt for the worm to live in. 'There, perfect, just the right home,' Marco said cheerfully. He gave the worm some pellets to eat. What he didn't know was something bizarre was going to happen.

The next day he woke up and the worm was gone! Luckily it was Saturday so he went down to the front yard to find it. He went outside and found the longest, slimiest, ugliest thing he had ever seen. *It was an oversized worm!*

The worm went to attack but Marco dodged. He zoomed to Dr Hibbert to see if there was a cure for this school project *gone wrong!*

'W-what can I use to stop this?' Marco asked curiously.

Dr Hibbert gave him the tablets and Marco ran home. When he got home the worm had eaten the garden hedge.

'Eat this loser!' shouted Marco and chucked the tablets at the worm and something amazing happened!

The worm shrunk. Marco looked down and saw the worm squiggle away. *Well that's my school project gone and it certainly went wrong*, he thought.

Ben Smallbone (11)
Greatham Primary School, Liss

THE ROOM 13

Today was the first day of term at Lake Valley High, my new secondary school. The wind was blowing in my bright ginger hair, the grass was so beautiful it was shining. My friend Anne was shouting my name. 'Ashley, Ashley come over here.'
I went to go and see what the matter was. Anne was standing by the school notice board. 'Look, look you room is 13 for your tutor classes.'
'This is so unfair,' I said at lunch. 'Why do I always get the bad luck?'

That afternoon I went into my room 13. No one was there. Then all of a sudden I heard a noise . . . *bang!* The desk fell down. It was a black cat! 'Black cats are unlucky,' I screeched. The cat crept closer then it pounced. My heart pounded, my legs shook like jelly, I felt sick! The cat came for me and bit me. Blood poured out gallons and gallons. There was a huge pile of blood on the floor. I screamed, *'Argh!'*

Next week I went back in, this time it was a ladder, I was forced to go underneath, then it fell on me. I was told that I had been knocked out and it took me three weeks to recover!

The night I came out of hospital I heard this, 'Ashley I'm on the first step. I'm coming to get you, beware!'

I then found out that Anne got 13 and I got lucky 4!

Hannah Panton (10)
Greatham Primary School, Liss

MY BROTHER'S BIRTHDAY PARTY

My brother's fifth birthday was last week, his name is Matt. Oh how hectic it was! Thirty little five year olds running about the house and garden destroying anything in their path. When it came to food we thought that a multipack of tissues was enough but of course so many faces got mucky and so many drinks were spilt we had to get some more.

People looked at my mum and exclaimed, 'She must be crazy taking on thirty children.' But Mum just smiled and walked away. Finally it was sleeping lions and they were all that tired that they fell asleep. I was playing too and I fell asleep. I went upstairs to my room. There were thirty children ripping out my drawers and putting shorts on their heads and dresses around their ankles.

I screamed out, *'Muummm!'* suddenly thirty kids started to wail.

'Now, now what's going on?'
'Well they were all in my room messing it up.' Suddenly I thought, *yes they're going, yes, yes, yesssss!* but Matt stayed and that lot went forever and never came back.

Nicole Holbrook (11)
Greatham Primary School, Liss

THE MUMMY

It was the year of 1922 and Howard Carter was looking all over for Tutankhamen's tomb, he also had one Egyptian helper called Mat. They were digging for five years then they found it, King Tutankhamen's tomb. But there were steps and that took one year to unbury. Finally they did.

'How long's it been?' said Mat.

'Only seven years and I'm going in first,' said Howard Carter.

So he did.'*Wwwwaaahhhooo* look at all that gold, it's lovely,' he shouted.

'Yep it's shiny,' said Mat, 'and it's mine.'

'No it's not Howard, it's the King's.'

'But he's dead,' said Howard but then the tomb rocked side to side and there was a banging noise on every wall then . . . it was silent.

'By the way, where is Tutankhamen's body?'

'I don't know do I,' answered Howard.

Five weeks later they were so hungry they took a bit out of something mouldy, it was Tutankhamen's body.

'Sir, what is this?' said Mat.

Howard opened his eyes. 'A body. Run and hide Mat.'

So they did, but the mummy found Howard and sucked his life out of him. Howard was dead and the mummy was half human. Then Mat found Howard and thought it was the King. '*Yyyesss* he's dead.' Then Mat got stabbed and fell to the ground and Tutankahmen sucked his life out of him.

Now Tutankhamen was human and ruled Egypt again.

Sophie Pullen (11)
Greatham Primary School, Liss

A Day In The Life Of . . . Aragorn/Strider

6.30am

I have woken up to a nice day with the good old bread and mutton. I'm having a quick rest before I go through Fangorn. It sounds dangerous but there's the life of a ranger for you. I am hoping to see an Enth. I had better go now.

7.45am

I have seen an Enth. I don't think he has seen me. Wait a minute, it's moving towards me, better move. *Bang!* that was close, it almost stepped on me. Wait a minute, it's an Enth cave.

8am

I have entered the cave. Here is a sword, there are ruins, I hope Elrond can read them.

8.15am

What's that sound? *Ambush!* I have slain many Orcs. I shall rest here tonight.

Thomas Brown (11)
Greatham Primary School, Liss

THE DEVIL

'One day when a boy called David went to post a letter, he did not come back! Where did he go? Nobody knows. What happened to him? Nobody knows. We will bring you another report on this bulletin in 15 minutes.'

'I wish I never sent him to post that letter,' said David's mum
'Well, we can't go back in time now can we?' said David's dad. 'I wonder what happened to him.'

The next day Dad rang the police force and the officer said, 'We will put our best detective on the case, Detective Holmes.'

It was Friday 13th May 2032 in the afternoon at 1500 hours and Detective Holmes rung David's doorbell. Mum answered the door and he said, 'Hello Detective Holmes at your service.' David's mum showed him to the living room and showed him a picture of David. 'I will do my best,' said Mr Holmes.

The next week Mr Holmes had just about solved the mystery. He said, 'There is a devil on the loose.' The next month they had caught the devil and it was a person in a Hallowe'en costume.

'Apparently,' said Detective Holmes, 'it was a madman that had escaped from a mental hospital! There is even more good news.'
'What's that?' said David's mum.
'David is alive and well.'

'The criminal behind this disappearing lark is behind bars,' the news reporter said.

James Horwood (10)
Greatham Primary School, Liss

CHANGING PARENTS

Tim was reading a book in class. The book was called 'Changing Parents'. Tim thought that if the story was real, it would be terrible.

When he got home, he told his mum about his day. When he told his mum about the story, she was puzzled, but laughing.

In the morning, when he was walking to school, near the gate, he thought he saw a ghost, *'Boo!'* shouted the ghost. It was weird, because it looked very like his dad. When he got into his class, he told all his best mates, but none of them believed him. He was really getting wound up. He was really spooked out, after the ghost, he was frightened to walk home.

That night at tea time, his mum asked him, 'How was your day dear?'
Tim replied, 'Spooky, I saw a ghost today.' His mum started laughing. She asked him if he had seen Dad today, he said, 'No,' (he was shaking).
His food turned into a ghost. 'Argh!' He ran up the stairs, into his bedroom and locked the door.

That night Tim woke up and went to his Mum and Dad's bedroom because he didn't feel well. But his parents were not there. He went downstairs, nothing was normal, it seemed like a haunted house. Tim was terrified, *'Arrgghh!'* he shouted. 'Mum, Dad! Where are you?'
The door slammed, his parents were gone.

Sam Trevor (11)
Greatham Primary School, Liss

MY DAY OUT

It was a lovely day. As we walked through the fields I could feel the warm breeze gently blowing through my hair. The sun shone on the river making the water sparkle. There were several people sitting along the river bank with their fishing rods. Meal worms were wriggling in little boxes as bait.

I peered into the rippling water and could see lots of tiny minnows. A family of swans paddled downstream. I could see the reeds moving in the middle of the river and noticed a nest amongst them. Ducks swam and dived for food.

As I gazed across the river I could see the ripening corn swaying in the gentle breeze. We were approaching a stile into the next field, where cows were grazing, when we spotted a kingfisher perched on a branch just above the water. I was really excited as I had never seen one before. It was unmistakable as it was a vivid blue. It dived into the water and flew back to the branch. It stayed for several moments and then was gone.

We sat and had lunch amongst the clover and the buttercups. I wrote down in my notebook all the things we had seen as we'd walked through the fields. I didn't want to forget anything, especially the kingfisher.

Emma Downes (9)
Hill View Primary School, Bournemouth

SPOOKY SHADOWS

It was a cold, dark night as I entered the woods. The only light came from the full moon shining down from the midnight sky. As I walked through the trees, I stood on the dead leaves as they crunched under my feet.

The night was silent, then an owl hooted on the branch of a tree. I stopped, I was scared. I suddenly heard a branch break behind me, I turned around, my heart was beating like a drum. *Boom, boom, boom, boom!* There was nothing behind me, the owls tooted again making my heart beat even faster. I had to walk through the woods, I kept on going. The tall trees stood still like statues with spooky shadows. They seemed to move like wooden giants in the darkness. I looked up at the moon. It was light and bright. I felt afraid. I heard twigs snap and small footsteps behind me. I looked back but I didn't see anything.

I began to shiver and shake, I felt as cold as ice. I pulled my hood over my head to keep warm. The wind was getting stronger, I could hear the wind whistling through the trees. I started to walk faster in the woods. I wanted to get home. The trees began to move in the wind, they were just like big monsters. I looked behind me. I could hear lots of noises. I thought I could hear someone whispering but the strange thing about it was nobody was there.

Through the trees I could see my house. I was getting closer to home. I could see lights on in front of the door. I just ran and ran and ran until I got to my front door. My heartbeat had stopped drumming. I put the key in the door and kicked it with my foot. The door swung open, then I ran inside and slammed the door shut *bang!* I felt relieved to be back home.

Elliot Smith (9)
Hill View Primary School, Bournemouth

MEDAL OF HONOUR

1941 seven hundred soldiers took front line. Four soldiers were picked to go behind enemy lines. Twenty were chosen to cover fire those four soldiers. The Germans or Nazis raided the beaches of Normandy. Two hundred more reinforcement soldiers came to back up front line. Commando Lieutenant Dan led six hundred troops into battle. The firing three hundred troops killed two bunkers of Nazis. Six hundred troops turned into five hundred and ninety troop. Ten were killed in the advance. Two German panzars were destroyed in the battle. Dan took charge of ten American field guns. Another three were cleared, all bunkers cleared. All soldiers were picked up and brought back to ship. Unfortunately a squadron of Focke-Wolfs was at full pelt at HMS Sheffield. The squadron did make a big fire but it was put out in two minutes.

The ship went to two different places. The first place was Southampton docks for food supplies and Poole Bay for fuel. But when the ship reached halfway point paratroopers invaded the ship and tried to take it back to Germany but Dan told them the wrong directions and instead of them being prisoners the Germans were prisoners.

Peace was declared in America and Britain.

Daniel Joy (9)
Hill View Primary School, Bournemouth

CHARLOTTE'S THEME PARK

It was great. We were off in the car at 8am on our way to Charlotte's theme park. We got there in no time at all, it looked really good. The first ride I went on was The Zoom. It was really fast and exciting. I went on another ride and it shot up and suddenly dropped, I was really frightened.

Then my tummy rumbled so I had some lunch, I had a chocolate cookie, some donuts and a prawn salad with lots of chocolate. I went on a water ride and a roller coaster. They were really fun but I got drenched. Then suddenly I heard my mum calling, I woke up. It was all a dream.

I went to school the next day and told my friends about my adventure and went to the school fête, it wasn't as good as my dream though!

Charlotte Palmer (9)
Hill View Primary School, Bournemouth

ELOISE AND THE MAGIC SNAKES

Once upon a time, there was a little girl called Eloise. She had long blonde hair and pink skin.

She went into the deep dark woods and found a snake. At first, she thought it was a normal snake but it spoke to her, saying, 'I am a magic snake. If you stay with me, nothing at all will hurt you.'

She went on walking with the snake through the woods. Suddenly, a huge, fierce lion came darting towards them. Eloise started to run away but the snake cried, 'No! don't run away. I will stop him.' He slithered around a little and hissed loudly, and the lion scampered away whimpering.
'Wow!' exclaimed Eloise. 'That was amazing.'

The snake said, 'Do you want to meet my friends? They can grant you five wishes, make you fly and see into the future. We are all amazing.'

So they went into the snake cave. The one Eloise liked best was a black snake called Zachary who had red spots and green stripes. He made her fly right across the cave. There was also a big, fat snake who granted her five wishes, which was very useful.

After quickly wishing for the usual things - money, a boyfriend, exotic holidays and a self-cleaning house - Eloise pondered a little about her last wish.

Eventually it came to her. An enormous ice cream cone to carry all those magic snakes home, as they might come in handy one day . . .

Sophia Jackson (9)
Hill View Primary School, Bournemouth

ZELDA AND HER SPELLS

One spooky night, the day just before Hallowe'en, Zelda the witch wasn't ready because all of the spells she was supposed to do she did wrong. Example, when she wanted her cat to fly it changed colour. The headmaster of all witches came along and saw Zelda saying her spells wrong.

The headmaster was called Zoomby, he wore large, heavy boots and a huge, black cape. He was very tall and he had white frizzy hair and a long, white, curly beard. He could be kind but sometimes if we didn't do our spells right he was a bit nasty. Zelda asked Zoomby for some help.
Zoomby said, 'You have to work your spells out yourself.' Zoomby strolled out of the room.
Zelda kept practising her spells at night, and at last she did one spell right. She was so happy she told Zoomby.
He said, 'Congratulations Zelda.'

Hallowe'en arrived, Zelda was able to do all the spells she wanted to do because she had been practising. She collected her broom and cat and flew off to show all of the other witches because all of the witches knew Zelda couldn't do any of her spells right, but she proved them wrong. She was better than all of her other witches at doing her spells because she practised all night. Zelda showed all the other witches how to do some spells that they couldn't do, she was the best witch out of all of the other witches because they thought they were better than Zelda but they were not. If you practice you will eventually get it right like Zelda.

Hollie Reeves (9)
Hill View Primary School, Bournemouth

UNTITLED

One night in bed the clock chimed 2am. I had been lying awake all this time. I began to smell something old and musty. In the corner I noticed a mist coming towards me. As it got closer I saw it was a man with large teeth. I shot under my pillow shivering. I said to myself, 'It's a vampire!' I could hear my teeth chattering. I tried to pull myself together.
Next moment he touched my head, he said, 'Get up.'
I slid out of my bed, he took my hand, we flew through the window, over the house tops. I was frightened to breathe in case I fell. What did this vampire want? Suddenly we landed with a crash to the ground. I was not hurt. I could not scream, my mouth was dry. We began to walk across the field. I fell down a large well turning and tossing. I thought, *I have lost the vampire.*

I landed at the bottom, crashing my head on something hard. I touched my head, I knew there would be blood. I could feel heavy breathing on me and something was shaking me. My thought was, *he's back.*

I opened my eyes and saw my mum leaning over me, I hadn't fallen down the well, I had fallen out of bed and hit my head. It was just a nightmare!

The moral of this story is *don't have cheese for supper.*

Anthony Stratton (8)
Hill View Primary School, Bournemouth

FAIRIES

Long, long ago there was a castle made of shining white teeth, which the magic fairies had made.

One night I looked out of my glass window and was surprised to see fairies playing on the green grass. There were five little fairies with blonde hair like a sheet of silk and small wings made of gossamer. They looked so dainty dancing in the silvery moonlight.
'Hello Kirsty, do you know where our friend Lily is? She's missing, please come with us to the park to help us find her,' said the fairies.
'Yes of course I will come,' replied Kirsty.

Kirsty grabbed her shopping basket and all of the fairies jumped into it. We walked down the dark street, finally reaching the park. The fairies jumped out of the basket to find Lily.

Eventually I found her hiding under a daisy. She was crying so I picked her up and gave her a cuddle. I called over the fairies and they all gave Lily a hug. When she stopped crying she explained that a cat had chased her. So then I picked them all up and took them home.

Kirsty Read (9)
Hill View Primary School, Bournemouth

THE POISON FACTORY

Long ago there lived two children called Amy and Zac. Amy was ten with long brown hair and blue eyes that sparkled like diamonds. Zac was also ten and had spiky brown hair with chocolate-brown eyes that glisten in the sunlight. They lived in Scotland, high up on a hill in a unique cottage.

One day Amy and Zac went to the shop and took a short cut. When they were walking through a narrow, pebbly path Zac noticed an abandoned barn. So they went to look inside. They cautiously opened the door and crept in. They were in a poison factory.

Suddenly a man leapt out and grabbed Zac and took him upstairs. Amy ran for her life, she went up the hill and home again.

When Amy got home she immediately rang the police and said, 'Please come quick, a stranger has snatched my best friend.'

In one minute the police had arrived and Amy led them to the barn. The police quickly realised they were selling illegal poison and were desperate to find the stranger. The police scrambled up the stairs and caught the man. They soon arrested the man and drove Zac and Amy home in the safe hands of their mother and they lived happily ever after.

Rachael Ainsworth (9)
Hill View Primary School, Bournemouth

THE LIFE OF DAVID BECKHAM

Starting from when he was little, David Beckham's dream was to play for Manchester United. One Christmas David got a Man Utd shirt from his mum but his grandad got him a Tottenham shirt! David still said, 'Thank you,' and he wore it every time he visited his grandad.

He got older and older, and his dream was still the same. One day he did play for Manchester United and he was number ten. He scored goals, sat on the bench and he set up goals with his fantastic right foot, and then he met Victoria after a game, with the Spice Girls. David and Victoria got married a couple of months later and had two children, Brooklyn and Romeo.

In the season '02 to '03 (which Beckham was number seven) he had a brilliant season in the Premiership and he had lots of talks to go to Real Madrid, AC Milan or Barcelona, but in the end he accepted Real Madrid's contract and he's there now with some of the greatest players in the world.

He won lots of trophies at United, now let's hope he wins lots at Madrid. A lot of people are unhappy and upset about Beckham's departure, but it is just life. The England skipper has great memories in the number seven shirt but how many memories will he have in the number eleven or twenty-three shirt for Real Madrid?

Harrison Shaw (10)
Hill View Primary School, Bournemouth

SOPHIE . . . THE GHOST

You'll never guess just where I've been. Perhaps I should start right from the beginning.

Well, one beautiful day (as all tales start) I, Jace Kane, was outside sunbathing when along came what I thought was my brother in a sheet . . . but boy, I was very surprised when he walked through my house without opening a door, or a gate for that matter!

I raced after this thing desperately panting. After five minutes I caught up with this brother-like thing and shouted, 'Oh you!'
There was a young girl's reply, 'Yes, what do you want from me?'
'Who are you?'
'Sophie Chelly.'
'How old are you?' I curiously asked.
'Well, I'm not being rude,' she began, 'but I'm dead.'
I panicked, how could this be? Then it suddenly came to me . . . *she's a ghost,* I thought and to follow, as if by magic, as quick as a flash I was zapped onto a small but heavenly island.
I asked daringly, 'Where am I, I mean, where are we?'
Sophie Chelly explained, 'You guessed that I was an angel, I mean ghost, well oh I've let a bit loose but the fact is you guessed I was a ghost therefore you are to stay on Hullabaloo Island. You'll be treated very fairly, don't worry.'

I wept quite hard then . . . 'But I've got a home to go to, a family!' I got frustrated.
'OK, OK,' Sophie gave up. 'I'll try to smuggle you out!'

The next day Sophie hid me under her coat and flew me gently home.
'Thank you,' I cried as I went inside.

That night I dreamt about Sophie and thought if I could repay her in any way I would. She made me very happy!

Jace Kane (10)
Hill View Primary School, Bournemouth

A Day In The Life Of My Brother

One day, I woke up and felt different, drunk and most of all, older. I climbed clumsily out of bed and looked at my legs. 'They've grown hairy,' I said coldly to myself. I wasn't sure whether it was my body creating the new me, so I plodded downstairs for breakfast.

'Morning Mum,' I said to my mother as I slowly entered the kitchen.

'Morning dear,' she replied. 'Why were you up clubbing last night, David? You know how we worry.'

'B-but, I wasn't clubbing last night. I was in bed at 7 o'clock and my name's not David!' I said, astonished.

'Oh, come on dear, you're hardly your seven-year-old brother, Simon, tell me the truth. Were you clubbing last night or not?'

I walked out the room. I was beginning to get stressed when suddenly I heard some tiny footsteps coming down the stairs. A boy about my age and height walked past.

'Hi,' he whispered, 'something weird's happening. I don't feel the same as usual.'

'I know, Mum keeps calling me David when I'm not. Who are you anyway?' I asked puzzled.

'I'm David, idiot. You should of seen that when you looked at me. I mean, you're not seven, so pull yourself together,' he replied.

'The problem is, I am seven. Are you sure you're David? You don't look it to me.' As soon as I said this I felt a spark of blazing fire hit my arm and I didn't feel old anymore. I didn't feel tired. I felt myself again.

Alice Smith (10)
Hill View Primary School, Bournemouth

WHO WANTS TO BE DIFFERENT OR LIKE SOMEONE ELSE?

Buffy the vampire slayer got up ready to have another day of adventure. But she didn't know what she was letting herself in for, as her sister wanted to be more adventurous. So she looked in some of Buffy's books, well spell books and looked for a spell to give her powers. She went outside and read out what it said. Suddenly a demon raced round and grabbed Dawn and Buffy's book. Dawn got swept off her feet and crouched under a demon's arm.

Then as quick as a flash Buffy came racing round the corner with a stick and stabbed the demon in the stomach and it dissolved into dust. Buffy picked up the book 'Willow The Witch', Buffy's friend bumped into her and caught her at the wrong time. Willow took the spell book and gave Dawn a cross look. Willow went back inside with Dawn. Buffy went to look for more demons as sometimes Buffy doesn't need tools to be good as she is a slayer. She saw Faith and Kendra, they are both slayers as well. But she wanted to fight demons on her own, they didn't even take notice of her anyway.

'I'm going to get you even though you are the slayer, I am the Master,' shouted the evil man.
Buffy just stabbed him and he dissolved into dust. Dawn stared at Buffy as she walked away. There was no more demons and Dawn understood.

Charlotte Butler (9)
Hill View Primary School, Bournemouth

WILL IT GO WRONG?

Lisa was late for school again. She was up all night trying to arrange a disco. Lisa had to organise a disco for the school. She was the chosen one. It was Hallowe'en, so she had to decorate the hall with pumpkins and fake cobwebs and of course broomsticks. But Lisa had to buy all the decorations herself which she thought was very unfair. The trouble was they couldn't use their hall because they needed it to hold the stage for the school's plays. Where could they have the disco, where?

That day she walked round the school to see where else was big enough to have a disco.
'Claire, how about there? No, it's too small,' Lisa said to her friend.
'I know, outside!' Claire suggested seriously. 'We can have it outside, then it's dark and scary and more like Hallowe'en! We could hang candles.'

So it was arranged. They would have the disco outside for Hallowe'en. Lisa began the arrangements as soon as she told their teacher, Mrs Limpet.

Lisa had carved out the pumpkin faces, spread out the cobwebs, placed the broomsticks out and set out the food and drink two hours before the disco.

That night everything went well. The food and drinks were gone by the end of the disco. Lisa was exhausted by ten o'clock.
'Claire, I did it, nothing went wrong, apart from when I spilt cake down me!' The two girls giggled.
The disco was a complete success! Hooray!

Gemma Hayward (10)
Hill View Primary School, Bournemouth

THE PALE GHOST

I saw him just floating over my new bike. He was tall, thin and he sent a shiver down my spine. His face had blots of ink all over it. I thought he was dead or covered in white paint. His face was also pale, *he must be hungry* I thought. *Should I get him something to eat or not? Well I guess I could just get him a piece of marble cake.* I tiptoed into the kitchen, cut a piece of cake then scrambled out into the garden. I was shivering all over the place.

After a while I pulled myself together and held my hand out and gave the cake to him.
He stared at me strangely.
I said, 'What is your name?'
He replied, 'Punky, what's yours?'
'Maria Lopez.'
Punky held open his mouth and I threw the cake into it. He chewed it and he crunched it, then he swallowed it. You'll never guess what happened after he had swallowed it, it came out the other end!
I cried, *'Argh, you're a ghost!'* I ran out of the garage, into the house and went upstairs and screamed into a pillow.

The next day I thought I had to overcome my fear. I went into the garage. As soon as I set foot into the garage something scuttled across my bare feet, it was Punky.
I whispered, 'Would you like to be my ghoulfriend?'
'Yes please,' he shouted.

Hayley Jewell (10)
Hill View Primary School, Bournemouth

Lost Children

One fine summer's day, when the world was still young, there lived two children and their father and mother. The two children's names were Jack and Mary.

At lunchtime their mother and father said they could go into the woods and take a picnic lunch. So off they went, over hedges and trees until they came to the woods. There they found a lovely wide open space to have a picnic.

After lunch they decided to have a wander. They strolled through the trees and finally they ended up deep in the heart of the wood. Just then a wolf jumped out in front of them, staring with teeth as pointed as swords and eyes red and fire-like. It was as grey as the pavement. The children ran for their lives.

They soon came to two horses. Both had strong-looking men on top. Jack then told them their story. The riders agreed to help. So with one child on one horse and another child on another horse, they galloped round bushes, they galloped through trees (one narrowly missing Mary's head) until they came to a clearing. The children jumped off, one by one said farewell and left.

Soon they were getting near home when they met the wolf. The wolf quickly said he was a nice wolf and he knew the way home for he had passed it before, so they all agreed that the wolf should take them home.

When they got there, their parents were so worried that they said they would never let them out on their own again. But they met the wolf and he said he would be their friend forever. So they all lived happily every after.

Matthew Shore (9)
Hill View Primary School, Bournemouth

THE BAD VIKING

On the 8th June AD793, the Vikings raided Lindisfarne. It was going very well for the Vikings, the monks were running away and were not fighting, but it was not going well for one Viking. His name was Ragnar. He was a young Viking and when he got out of the longboat he knew there would be trouble. He was right, when he got out off the boat, he tripped over a rock and landed head first in the water. When he got up he was drenched but kept fighting. Ragnar charged at a monk and looked at his belt to get his sword but it had fallen out when Ragnar fell in the water. By the time he looked up the monk had gone.

After the Vikings raided Lindisfarne they went back home to Norway. When Radnar's ship got in to the dock he was not very happy. He said to himself, 'I'm very clumsy.'

The next morning Ragnar went to the church to pray to Odin and Thor, today Ragnar was going to pray to Odin.
Ragnar said to Odin, 'Please help me, I'm clumsy and I want to be good at fighting.'
Then the floor began to shake and the middle of the church began to crack and lightning flashed all over the church and then Odin said, 'Your wish is accepted.' And it was all quiet.

The crack in the floor was gone and the shaking had stopped. Ragnar went back home and in each battle Ragnar went to, he was very, very fierce.

Reece Smith (9)
Hill View Primary School, Bournemouth

THE HAUNTED HOUSE

Deep in the woods their was an old, derelict house, it was said that the house was haunted by ghosts.

One day I was walking through the woods with my two friends Robert and McCawley. It was a bright sunny day, we sat down on a tree stump, we had lunch together.

At 8 o'clock when we stopped playing we realised it was starting to get dark, we decided we should go home.
I turned to Robert and said, 'Which way is it?'
'I don't know, ask McCawley.'
McCawley said, 'You know don't you?'
'No!' I said.

So I lead them through the woods, we came to a spooky house. We walked up the twisted path, and came to a huge door. To our surprise the door opened and we walked in, we walked up the stairs and something flew past me laughing. It was a ghost, so we ran out through the door, down the path and through the woods and kept on running until we reached home.

Adam Lugrin (9)
Hill View Primary School, Bournemouth

LIZARD LAND

Hi I'm Lewi and this is my story of the evil lizard land I entered when I crashed in space!

It all started when the navigation system went horribly wrong. I crashed onto a fiery red planet, which seemed deserted. I was wrong! There were lizards, dragons and all the reptiles you could imagine! Two alligators dragged me by my shaky legs and took me to a massive dragon. It had a baby alligator in his grip and was killing it! When he finished eating it, he let out a huge roar that blasted me onto the floor. I picked myself up.
The dragon roared, 'You must die, you cannot leave this planet.'

I turned and ran as fast as I could. An army of snakes rose from the ground and followed me. I bumped into something, it was my partner Jake. 'Run as fast as you can!' I yelled.
We ran and ran. At last we lost the snakes, and both collapsed. Moments later I heard thunderous footsteps, I looked up and saw four robot lizards. We were too tired to fight, they carried us to a laboratory.

Inside they strapped us to metal tables and injected us with a potion. We were told this was the only way to stay alive, we were being turned into reptiles. They then set us free.

We found our way back to our ship, and are sending this message in hope someone will rescue us - position unknown.

Lewis Nicholls (9)
Hill View Primary School, Bournemouth

THE LEGEND OF THE ANCIENT DRAGON

It was an unusual day in the middle of autumn. The children were playing in the middle of the planet Goptra when suddenly . . . the ghost of an ancient dragon swept the countryside boiling and tossing sheep into its mouth.

After many years of sheep-napping, the wizard known as Mr Kasaki came and tried to challenge the ancient dragon. The ancient dragon gave an evil cackle and agreed. The wizard leapt forward ready to attack when the dragon gave off a giant sneeze and blew the wizard away. Thinking he had won, the dragon began to lie down and sleep!

The wizard returned with many other mystical creatures and tried to turn the dragon into a tiny mouse which could easily be beaten. But, the dragon woke and gave a terrible roar which frightened the creatures away leaving Mr Kasaki helpless and alone to face the evil ancient dragon with only a single spear.

Mr Kasaki threw the spear and prayed it would hit the ancient dragon. The ancient dragon fell to the ground. It was now dead! Mr Kasaki was a hero!

Jonathan Aldridge (10)
Hill View Primary School, Bournemouth

HOUSE OF THE DEAD

There was a house in a village called Golden Valley, the most fancy house you could think of. This was the most deadly house ever, so far twenty people had died, they were not in a good state when they died. Their big and small intestines were hanging out, the faces were cut, never a pretty sight.

A new family came to live in Golden Valley, but the bad thing was that they were in the house of the dead.

On the first night the family of four were watching TV when for no reason the TV turned off. They tried to turn it back on but it didn't. This was the first time they trembled. The two parents told their two children to go to bed. Jenny and Phillip went to bed. They fell straight to sleep.

Phillip was the first to wake up, but it wasn't morning it was twelve o'clock, he heard banging of drawers. He got out of bed, walked down the hallway and went into the room.

Jenny was woken up by a terrifying scream. She walked into the room and tripped over to see Phillip was dead and she saw a ghostly figure, and she was petrified.

Robbie Treadwell (10)
Hill View Primary School, Bournemouth

THE BEAUTIFUL STALLION

A long time ago there lived a beautiful stallion, he lived in the country in a large field. When the day was bright his lovely black coat shone in the sun. His name was Harvey and his owner Molly was quite mean, funnily enough Harvey was the best horse you could dream of, or was he?

Molly had a friend called Micky who sometimes looked after Harvey and that's when the trouble started!

Molly had asked Micky if she could look after Harvey while she went on holiday, Micky agreed to the above plans after some persuading. When Molly went to say goodbye before she left, she was talking to Harvey and started to say, 'Don't worry I'll be back soon and Micky's going to look after you so you be a good boy.'
All Harvey was thinking was, *hooray, now the chance to have some real fun, I wonder what I could do?*

After a few days of thinking Harvey decided what to do, he would run away, and so he did in the middle of the night!

The next day Micky went to the field and found Harvey gone! 'Oh no, I'll have to phone Molly to say that he is gone. What have I done,' Micky said in dismay. Of course it wasn't Micky's fault, after an hour or two she phoned Molly up, she wasn't going to come back so she called a search party but there was no need because he was munching on food in the tack room, it was such a relief.

Georgina Moore (10)
Hill View Primary School, Bournemouth

HORROR HOUSE 3

One day five teenagers had an idea to spend a vacation in Horror House 3! They saved their money up and eventually had enough to go to Horror House 3.

It was a sunny Friday afternoon when they all met at the park to add up their money. Brad had £720, Katy had £699, Joe had £729, Shelly had £730 and Tom had £591. They had enough.

They all went home to pack their stuff and get their passports. They all met back at the airport to check in. They heard someone say that the next plane left in 10 minutes. They couldn't stop laughing on the way there because they were all watching Mr Bean, well except for Tom, he was asleep.

Well time passed quickly and they were in Spain. I suspect their hearts were beating like drums. The first night was uneventful but the second night was fantastic. Suddenly the people who appeared to be dead jumped out, this was all a big set up.

They all went downstairs for tea and talked about the best vacation ever. When they had all been home for about a month they all decided to visit Horror House 3 every year.

Dean Brown (10)
Hill View Primary School, Bournemouth

THE TERRIFYING GHOST

I saw him, the white, floating, scariest ghost you have ever seen. I had only just moved house, I was exploring and that is when I saw him. I saw him in the garage, he was pale and very hungry. My mum said he was fake but my dad said he was real. I do not know what to do, I want to take him to see my friends but I'm not sure they will think he is real, they might think he is a joke. He is very scary but my mum says he must stay but my dad says he must go. I ran, I was terrified, all the way back into the old broken house and I told my mum. She said she already knew there was one ghost.

Suddenly the doorbell went and it was one of my friends. I panicked and I ran out of the house and into the garage but my friend ran after me. When he got to the garage he ran, I had about fifty-one ghosts behind me, they followed me, I ran into my room. They had come out of the garage they started fading, it was over.

Kelsey Green (8)
Hill View Primary School, Bournemouth

BIG FOOT RABBIT

Have you ever heard of Big Foot Rabbit? His teeth are huge and his tail is tiny.

One day (like all fairy tales start) there was a little three-year-old girl who had only just moved house. She loved her old house. Her mum had just got her a new rabbit. Oh and I forgot to mention her name was Molly.

Molly wanted to get her rabbit out and her mum had said no. So off she went into the garden and got the rabbit out and dropped it. Molly had hurt his foot, but he was OK. The rabbit hopped along and went and hid. Molly couldn't find him, she looked all day. At 8 o'clock she still hadn't found him. She went into her mum and explained.
'Mum?' said Molly.
'Yeah, what's the matter? You look worried.'
'I can't find Harry.'

So her mum came out and tried to find Harry. They found Harry under the bench, but where Molly had dropped him he had a stone in his foot. Molly and her mum took Harry to the vet's.
'Argh! It's Big Foot. I have heard of him and I have been told never to treat him, take him away please.'
So off they went home but luckily Molly's mum was able to get the stone out. He was fine again.

The next day Molly wanted to get Harry out, but Harry would not let her. Molly muttered to herself, 'I wish I never had Harry. I wish I could sell him.' And from that day on she regretted every word of what she said.

Stephanie Jones
Hill View Primary School, Bournemouth

THE SCHOOL TRIP

It was time for Tower View School to go on their annual school trip to an old Victorian house. The house was called Misty Hill Hall.

The usual crowd, Clive, Lee and David were sat at the back of the coach laughing and throwing paper bullets at the girls. By midday they had arrived and settled in and were collecting wood for the evening BBQ.

'You know that this house is haunted don't you?' said Lee.
'Yeah right, and pigs might fly,' laughed Clive.
'I am not so sure. Shall we go back?' said David looking rather white.

At that point they heard a rustling in the bushes. The three boys could see a figure of a man walking ahead of them in the distance.
David screamed with fright.
Clive said, 'It's only Mr Jackson, our maths teacher.'

The figure moved slowly away. Then behind them they heard the voice of Mr Jackson. 'Come on boys.'

They were all frightened now, as the figure disappearing ahead of them wasn't Mr Jackson after all!

Curtis Jefferies (9)
Hill View Primary School, Bournemouth

TEAM EXTREME

Once there were some peace fighting heroes called Monkey Man, Sabre, Shadow, Dragon Lord, Stingerwasp and Sly Snake, and their enemy Dragonor, Lord of Destruction. He was the one who killed their master, just after he created them. Now they plan our vengeance for peace. Only then will the balance on Earth be even. Dragonor has razor-sharp claws and venomous fangs and the only thing to cure the venom is a big fat, sparkly diamond inside Dragonor's stomach.

It all started when they went to Mount Munkini where Dragonor lived, where the acid traps and spike bombs were made for evil. As they walked into the Mount Munkini it was guarded with element ninjas, there were thunder ninjas, fire ninjas, water ninjas, earth ninjas, wood ninjas, wind ninjas and Monkey Man said, 'I'll get the thunder, fire and earth ninjas, Sabre can help me, the rest of you get the rest.'
Then without a warning the ninjas started to attack. Sabre just managed to dodge two waist knives and a sword.

Finally Monkey Man killed the last one. Then they went in the cave and came face to face with Dragonor the Destructor who clouted Monkey Man across the room and poisoned Monkey Man with his spike. Then Sly Snake said, 'No one is allowed to poison my friend,' and thumped Dragonor across the room. Dragonor gave a thunder clap of a roar but before Dragonor could do anything Stingerwasp and Sly Snake killed Dragonor with a flying kick and stole the crystal which healed Monkey Man.

Andrew Dao (10)
Hill View Primary School, Bournemouth

THE ABANDONED DOGS

Suddenly I woke up from my silky cushion and my duvet was as velvety as feathery silk. Then I got dressed from my furry PJs and went downstairs to my breakfast. A spine-chilling shock went down to my toes . . . it was only the doorbell. I began to sneak up to the door and shouted, 'Hello Olivia!'
'Don't shout like that,' grumbled Olivia.
I stood, biting my lip, and then Olivia dragged me out the door heading towards school.

Suddenly we heard two loud puppy barks. We heard the crying in Parkstone, so we went to check it out. When we approached number 52, we saw a cute plump little face in the window. The door was unlocked so we went in to see the little dogs.

The state of the house was terrible, there was dogs' mess all over the floor. Carpets were ripped up, cans of beer were all over the cupboards then we saw a fire and fumes and puffs of smoke.
I shouted, 'We've got to get these dogs out and take them to my place!'
'OK,' Olivia said.

Suddenly, as quick as a flash, I took the two white ones and a black adult, Olivia took a golden retriever and a Dalmation.

Ten minutes later, I and Olivia scuttled home to wash and feed the animals and most of all, find them a family. After about a week of love and happiness, me and Olivia found homes for all of the dogs.
'You know Olivia, I can't think of a happier ending.'

Katie Gillett (9)
Hill View Primary School, Bournemouth

A DAY IN THE LIFE OF SPIDER-MAN

A day in the life of Spider-Man. First of all started off as Peter Parker and then there was an emergency and I got fitted into the Spider-Man suit. Then I started swinging building to building, the air was speeding past my ears and my web was dragging me across the city.

I finally saw the bad guy, it was the Green Goblin, he had got Mary Jane as well. I said, 'Let her go!'
Then he said that he'd make a deal, he would give Mary Jane back if he could rob a bank without me beating him up.
I said yes to the deal. He let her go but then I used my web and caught him, then I took him to a jail which he couldn't get out of. Even if he blew it up he wouldn't get out.

After that I went back to the house and became Peter Parker again. Then Mary Jane came round and I told her that I was Spider-Man and she gave me a little kiss on the cheek. Then Doctor Octopus smashed the wall and grabbed everyone, apart from me because I was in the toilet, I heard the screams and turned into Spider-Man and I smacked Doctor Octopus.

Joseph Wilcox (10)
Hill View Primary School, Bournemouth

THE WOODCUTTER'S FANTASTIC IDEA

Poppy woke with a start, the happy thought of letting a child into the world sent a surge of joy through her.

Poppy went through the woods to the market to buy the occasional bread and cheese for her twin children Lila and Lilo's lunch.

Harry Melbourne is a woodcutter. At home he was talking to Poppy, his wife. 'How can I make more money? Soon we might not even be able to afford the milk, cheese and bread for Lila and Lilo to eat, let alone us!'
'You'll think of something dear,' comforted Poppy.

At that moment Harry hugged his children, then his wife, grabbed his suitcase, a little money and what was left of the bread and cheese, he went to his shed and snatched up his tent.

A few hours later Harry arrived at the market on their horse and found a spot to put up his tent. The next morning Harry woke at 6.30am and went to get some wood and paint. By 9am he had made a table and 50 toys.

Just then a rich man came along and bought every toy for £200 for 20 weeks. By the end of 20 weeks Harry had £4,000. He returned to his house. They moved to a cottage in the country. Poppy had her baby, and named her Lala, so from that day onwards they were all happy.

Sian Flanagan (10)
Hill View Primary School, Bournemouth

THE GREAT ESCAPE

Abbey woke up with a flash, she was full of extreme excitement as today was the day that she went to summer camp. She had everything packed and ready, all Abbey's friends were going, like Jenny and Samantha, she couldn't wait.

Firstly Abbey had to feed her pet hamster Cubby. Hamsters were her favourite animal, they were so cuddly and cute. Abbey had breakfast her best cereal was Coco Pops.

Abbey and her mum drove off in the car, little did she know Cubby was gone!

Abbey had a great time at camp on her way back a strange feeling came over her. When she stopped telling her mum what she did she leapt upstairs, she ran into her room, suddenly she looked into the hamster's cage and had a massive shock. *Cubby was gone!* Abbey's face was filled with panic. Tears rolled off Abbey's diamond-blue eyes as she shut her door. She wept hysterically she looked in the places he might be.

Her mum came upstairs and said, 'What's the matter love?'

Abbey mumbled miserably, 'Cubby's g-gone.'

Abbey's mum's happy face turned into a terror-stricken face. They searched and looked everywhere. Abbey knew her cat Snowball was in the house as Cubby wasn't in her room, she started looking downstairs. She found the cat and guess who she found snuggled up next to that cat? Cubby! She ran and stroked him and the cat and always remembered to shut the cage door in the future.

Olivia Rogers (10)
Hill View Primary School, Bournemouth

THE NIGHTMARE

I woke up in the middle of the night wondering where I was. I looked around, I tried to shout but I couldn't. I tried to escape but I couldn't. Suddenly I saw something coming. I started to stare. I peered, I saw an alien. The alien came towards me. I tried to scream again but nothing came out. More and more were coming. I started to get dizzier and dizzier.
An alien called, 'Rebecca, Rebecca.'

They came closer and closer. Suddenly they grabbed my shoulder and I screamed. They walked back slowly.
I shouted, 'Where am I?'
'You're in space,' replied the alien. 'You're going to die!'
'No, no, no!' I screamed. They were getting closer and closer.

Suddenly I jumped out and fell down the hole. I was falling, falling. The aliens were calling and calling but I wasn't answering. They threw a rope down. I grabbed it and started to climb up and the aliens helped me up then I ran. They started to chase me.
Suddenly I fell and an alien said, 'Bye-bye, now you're going to die, ha, ha, ha!'
Suddenly I woke up and shouted, 'Where am I?' and my mum came in and put me back into bed. Everyone was fine.

Rebecca Johnson (10)
Hill View Primary School, Bournemouth

THE STRANGE DREAMS

Jana woke up in the middle of the night wondering where she was. She had been having strange dreams. She woke up because she was scared, her dreams were about vampires, ghosts and lots of other spooky things. She really wished that they would go away, but they wouldn't. Jana's dreams came every night, and every night she woke up frightened.

The dream came once again, and this is how it goes . . .

Jana was going down to her friends when suddenly she saw something coming towards her. She wasn't quite sure what they were because they had their backs turned, but suddenly they turned around. She was scared out of her wits. There were vampires, ghosts and ghouls, some of them she wasn't sure what they were, they just looked horrible. The ghosts were her family who had died a long time ago. They had come to haunt her. The vampires tried to suck her blood. The ghouls tried their hardest to catch her. They were getting closer and closer, it was as if they wanted her dead.

Jana started to run and run, as fast as she could, but more and more were coming after her, she ran down a lane but unfortunately it was a dead end. They all began to crowd around her when everything went black, they had got her . . . she felt something warm and furry by her face. She opened her eyes and saw that it was her cat. That's when she realised it had all been a bad dream and really she was at home in her nice warm bed.

Emma Hunter (9)
Hill View Primary School, Bournemouth

THE BIRTHDAY ON HALLOWE'EN

A young girl called Megan was about to celebrate her birthday on Friday 13th October. It was close to Hallowe'en, so her friends began to play the dangerous game of tricks and dares.

One day Mellisa, Megan's friend, had given her the most scary dare of them all - to go in the haunted house down Castle Road.

So that night Megan was trembling with fear as she walked down the dusty road, kicking any stones she saw. Megan could hear the whistling of the wind against the trees.

As she walked through the crooked old gates, the door had swung open for her. Megan's heart started beating like a band ready to start a show.

Then Megan had walked through the big iron door. Megan's mind started to play up. She could see shadows on the walls following her wherever she went. Then it began to come closer and closer and then she blinked and all was gone. She took a deep breath in and looked around.

She was beginning to cry as her heart swelled up inside her. Megan had opened her locket that her mother had given her when she was alive. Megan heard a creak by the door. She heard footsteps. Then suddenly it stopped.

She looked up and saw a . . .

Rosina Jacobs (10)
Hill View Primary School, Bournemouth

BEST FRIENDS

Jane and Kealy were best friends. Kealy was not so good at singing but Jane was. Jane wanted to be famous but Kealy didn't. Jane hated homework but Kealy loved it. The two girls didn't have a lot in common so they fell out. Now Jane and Sue are best friends and Kealy and Gemma are best friends too. Jane goes to singing lessons with Sue but she still likes Kealy and Kealy likes Jane - what should they do?

'I like having one best friend,' said Sally to Jane.
'Cos then you don't have to look out for six,' Sam said.
'You're wrong, I have loads of best friends then that way you don't fight,' Liz said proudly.
Jane thought for a moment, then ran to Kealy and Gemma.
'Listen, why can't me, you, Sue and Gemma all be best friends?'
'Umm! That would be too many,' Kealy answered.
'The more the merrier. You see having one best friend makes lots of fights and having lots doesn't,' Jane said kindly.
'Well, you're right but what will Gemma say?' wondered Kealy.
'I'll ask Sue, you ask Gemma,' Jane answered.

The girls asked Sue and Gemma and Sue said, 'Yes,' straight away but Gemma waited a minute and then said 'Yes!'

Now they're all best friends and play much more happily.

Lucy Gorst (9)
Hill View Primary School, Bournemouth

THE LEOPARD ON WHEELS

Thomas likes working on his branch line and Percy likes taking the mail. Gordon is the biggest and proudest engine and he likes pulling the Express but Henry loves the forest.

One day there was going to be an Animal Fair in the forest. Henry was sent to pick up some leopards. 'Peep, peep,' he whistled to Gordon. 'Henry, you're getting too excited and soon you're going to grow brown spots and a tail. Now a leopard on wheels, that would be exciting,' grunted Gordon.

Later Gordon was stuck at the bottom of the hill. He was waiting for Duck or Edward to help him up. Meanwhile Henry was collecting some monkeys. The leopards had come out of the trucks and were standing on the rails. The guard had gone for a walk.

The chains were old and one snapped. There was no guard to put on the brakes and the van chased the leopards down the hill, straight towards Gordon. All the leopards jumped on Gordon and scratched him and the brake van crashed into his face. Then James and Henry came to laugh at him.

'Now a leopard on wheels,' whispered Henry to James, 'is what Gordon would find exciting.'

At last Duck came to help him up the hill. Duck laughed at Gordon when he saw him.

Gordon had to go around with leopards climbing on him all day. At last the vet came and put the leopards back into their cattle truck.

The next day Gordon was going backwards to a water tower for a drink. He was telling Henry that he didn't find it exciting.

'Here's something else to find exciting,' called Henry as Gordon fell backwards into the turntable.

The Fat Controller arrived. 'Gordon you're not a leopard and you don't jump on turntables,' he said, 'now Henry will pull your train.'

Henry was delighted and puffed away at once.

Dominic Grace (9)
Hill View Primary School, Bournemouth

DOLPHIN DAYZ

In the Pacific Ocean, where dolphins live, the dolphins were playing - all except one. That one was very special. She wasn't like the other dolphins because she had magic eyes. Her eyes were in the shape of stars. No one liked her because she was different. Every year she would get to make a wish and it would come true. When that time of the year came, she knew what she wanted to wish for. 'I wish that all the other dolphins will play with me.' That was her wish.

The very next day the dolphin asked if she could play with the other dolphins, the reply was 'Yes!' So that day everyone was happy, they dived through the waves and jumped in the air and somersaulted. This was the best day of the dolphin's life.

Night soon came and the dolphins started to calm down. The nights were peaceful and in the ocean it was lovely. Soon the sun rose and every animal in the sea started to play. All the dolphins played together, and they all enjoyed playing together.

As the years passed, the magical dolphin made more wishes and the female dolphins had babies. The dolphin with the magical eyes had babies and they also had magical eyes, just like their mother. As more years passed by, more dolphins had babies and the babies in the family with the magical eyes, had them too. All the dolphins played together and loved each other.

Lauren Clarke (9)
Hill View Primary School, Bournemouth

THE FISHERMEN

Once there was a fisherman called Pete. Pete loved fishing but he was very greedy and selfish, he wanted to catch the biggest and best fish. Meanwhile his friend Emily was sitting on the side of the quay waiting for Pete to arrive so that they could fish together.

When Pete got to the quay, he said, 'I don't want to go fishing with you any more.'
'Why?' said Emily.
'Because I want to go by myself,' said Pete.
So Pete went to the next quay and he sat there by himself but he was very sad because he was all alone. He could see Emily and all their friends - Clare, Lisa and Jack, having fun, fishing together.

At the end of the day, Pete counted how many fish he'd caught, he only had eleven small, skinny fish and he'd had a very dull day. He strolled over to see how many fish his friends had caught. They had lots of big, fat, plump, juicy fish.

His friends asked how his day was and Pete said, 'My day was horrible, I only caught eleven fish and they're all very small.'
'I'm sorry to hear that you are so sad,' said Claire. 'Would you like to share our fish as we have lots?'
'Yes please,' said Pete, 'could we have a party and cook our fish for tea?'

So they all went back to Emily's house and had lots of fun playing together and eating all the fish they'd caught.

Rebecca Fish (8)
Hill View Primary School, Bournemouth

THE LONELY OLD WITCH

Ghostly howls were heard coming from the old battered house known as 'the haunted house'.

Nobody dared to go anywhere near the haunted house because a wicked old witch lived there.

Meanwhile the witch was busying making a potion to make herself look beautiful.

Three girls were standing by the gate watching the shadowy figure making spells. Suddenly there was a puff of smoke - the three girls ran.

The next day the girls were back. They dared each other to go into the house but they all said no at first, until the youngest said that she would. She went in and reached the living room without being noticed. The witch came hurtling down the creaky staircase and stood still in amazement. The girl screamed, her two friends waiting outside, ran away.

'I've always wanted a friend,' said the old lady.
The girl could picture all the things that the witch might do to her but the witch sat her down and gave her some food and a drink.
After that, she sent the girl home saying, 'I'm so lonely, living here on my own. All I need is a friend and someone to talk to.'
The girl could not believe what she was hearing.

She then left and walking down the lane to her house, she realised that the witch wasn't so bad after all and decided to return with her friends the very next day.

Louise Churchill (9)
Hill View Primary School, Bournemouth

THE UNEXPECTED

Far, far away in the land of Dorha there was a little village called Cowfarn. Just outside of the village was an old haunted, turreted house. No one dared to talk about the sinister house; no one even dared to whisper about it.

One evening, the clouds grew grey and the night became windy; the large castle gates were crashing and creaking against each other. The old lady's cat, Brato, found this very amusing. He was a tabby, an evil one, he had death written in each eye.

For the first time in years the old lady, Mrs MacMort, came out of her house in order to cast a spell on Cowfarn village. The wind grew stronger, there was a storm coming on. The people of the town were petrified. To make matters worse, the cat, Brato, went through each house scratching and biting everyone, so that the spell would work.

Suddenly the sun rose, its light unbearable for Mrs MacMort. She could not stand the light and shrivelled up so awkwardly, she had twisted into a ball.

She was put into a bottle and sent away - hopefully, she would never return.

Ciara Gill (9)
Hill View Primary School, Bournemouth

THE SPOOKY FACE

My name is Mark and I want to tell you about a weird event which happened last year. My mum and I live in an old, creepy house with creaking stairs. It was very scary for me and mum.

One night she woke up, looked in the mirror and a ghostly face stared right back at her. She screamed, 'What's happened to me? I've turned into a spooky monster!'

I ran quickly into her bedroom and saw for myself the ghostly image in the mirror. The face had spikes pointing out of its ears and the skin was scrunched up like a screwed up piece of paper.

When my mum turned around, her face was normal but the horrible ghost's face was still in the mirror. The ghost whispered in a gruff voice, 'Don't go away, help me please, I beg you. I've been trapped inside this mirror for 200 years. I can only be free if you smash the mirror then I can be happy again.'

My mum grabbed an old vase and threw it at the mirror which cracked into little pieces. 'Thank God that's over,' she said and we went back to bed, still shaking with fear.

The next day my mum bought a new mirror. I got up in the night and all of a sudden a young man's face stared back at me and whispered, 'Thank you for helping me.'

Was it all a dream?

Nathan Simpson (8)
Hill View Primary School, Bournemouth

HARRY POTTER IN THE LAND OF ALBERT SQUARE

Harry, Ron and Hermione started the walk from platform 1 to platform 9¾. As they pushed one after the other through the wall on the platform, they found themselves in a strange room and not on platform 9¾. Suddenly they heard a woman shout in a Cockney accent, 'Oi you get out of my pub, go on - clear off!'

Harry, Ron and Hermione were shocked.
Hermione said, 'We must have passed through a reverse reality spell.'
'Umm, we're very sorry but we've got a little lost. We were trying to get to Hogwarts,' said Harry. 'I'm Harry Potter, this is Ron and Hermione.'
'Oooh! Harry Potter, I've heard of you. Well I'm Gobby Mitchell and you're in Albert Square and I run the pub, The Three Broomsticks. I'll take you to the café, my son Phil Snape will 'elp you.'

Harry, Ron and Hermione went into the café. Pauline McGonagall and Ian Lockhart were sitting at a table.
''Ere! You're that Harry Potter!' said Pauline McGonagall. 'You're a bit lost then?'
'Just a bit,' said Harry.
'See Barry Broomstick Evans, he'll 'elp you,' said Phil Snape.

As they left, a boy bumped into Harry and glared at him, 'Watch it!' said Martin Malfoy.

Barry Broomsticks Evans sold Harry, Ron and Hermione, three second-hand broomsticks which they bought with money Harry had got from the Gringot's bank cash machine.

They were on their way to Hogwarts . . .

Adam Walker (8)
Hill View Primary School, Bournemouth

GOOSEBUMPS

One cold, stormy night, a beautiful young girl called Emma went for a walk for some fresh air.

Then her best friend Alice came out and said, 'Why are you out in the cold?'

'I just wanted to have a look in the window of the mask shop.' Then Emma sobbed and thought about her outfit for Hallowe'en. 'It's tomorrow night.' Her mum wanted her to wear the chick suit she had made for her.

'It's getting chilly, I'll see you tomorrow at school, bye!'

Emma started to walk home and then went fast asleep.

'Cookalookaloo!' went the cuckoo, always waking Emma up.

'Oh no, I'm late for school.' She missed the school bus and got detention for being late.

'Arrgghh!' screamed Emma, (Josh and Mat must have put a worm in her sandwich again). Emma ran off, pouring out with tears. Then she stopped crying and remembered about Hallowe'en night.

The mask shop was open, she went in and asked the man who owned the shop if she could buy one of the masks. He said, 'Yes, you can but you're not allowed those in that room.' The man then got a phone call and quickly Emma sneaked into the room and touched the masks and said to herself, 'This will scare Josh and Mat away.'

'Put that mask down now!' yelled the man.

Emma ran as fast as she could with the mask still in her hand.

The man shouted, 'Never bring it back!'

Emma got home and tried it on, it looked really scary but her little brother snatched it off her and he put it on but when he wanted to take it off, it wouldn't come off! His sister told him to stop being silly she took the mask off him and then went to find Alice.

Emma put the mask on and suddenly she started to talk differently and started being horrible to other people. She heard Josh and Mat playing pirates in the woods then she started to scare them and run after them.

After they had gone, Emma began to laugh then she stopped and tried to take the mask off but it wouldn't come off. When she got it off she ran into the woods and buried it.

The rest of the masks ran after Emma and she couldn't get away from them. She went back to ask the man at the shop to get them away from her even though the shop was shut.

The man let her in and said, 'I cannot help you because they're alive, they now have your body and they will not leave you alone. I can tell you one thing though, think from your heart and not your brain.'

She thought for a minute then went back into the woods, the masks were right behind her and as fast as she could she got the masks and brought them out of the ground and said, 'This is you, not me!' She was so desperate to be free. Then they disappeared and Emma went to Alice's house and Alice took Emma home and she went fast asleep.

Paige Benham (9)
Hill View Primary School, Bournemouth

A DAY IN THE LIFE OF CHEEKY

Hooray! I can hear Mum moving around upstairs. Any minute now, she'll come down and uncover my cage. Then I'll be able to tuck into my breakfast, probably seeds again! That's it, covers off! *Hop, hop, flap, flap,* must be quick. If my pal Smokey gets there first, he'll eat the lot. It won't enter his birdbrain to leave any for me. Good! David's eating his breakfast too. His sure looks tasty!

Mum's in the shower, now is my chance to have some fun. If I dash up and down on my perch screeching loudly, I know that David will let me out. Yep! It works every time. Come on Smokey, fancy stretching your wings? Race you to the curtain top.

Mum can't reach us up here so she'll have to take David to school and leave us free to play. I can fly back to the cage to sleep when I'm tired.

Uh oh, David's home! Hey, I'm not having that! Get your hands out of my house. *Peck, peck,* go on, get away! That made him move. Tasting David's fingers has made me peckish I think I'll just nibble some millet.

It sounds like Dad's arrived. Time for funny faces and silly noises through the bars. I wonder if he knows how childish he seems?

It's dinner time for the family now. I can see the sun going down outside. This will be my last chance for a fly today. Dad's covering me up now. I must chirp goodnight.

David Gower (9)
Hill View Primary School, Bournemouth

SLIMY

'How terrible!' cried Mrs Clark whilst watching the news. 'That can't be true. The three world's greatest scientists can't just have vanished!'

Mr Clark said nothing. The two adults were joined by Suzy and Mark, silent and still as a wall, in their corner.

'Experts are puzzled by these disappearances,' blasted the TV.
'It's rumoured that scientists were about to announce an important discovery in their work on whether calcite from African snail slime could be used to mend broken bones in humans.'

Suzy and Mark stared curiously at the TV and stirred slightly.

The night was dark and dismal as Mr Clark crept to the Science Lab. Now was his chance to steal the secrets of the snail slime, knowing that his colleagues had been dealt with.

A week ago he had been told he had lost his job as Chief Naturalist, so he had had to keep some of the lab's snail collection himself. He was still angry and jealous as he grabbed the files from the moonlit office. He turned sharply and stumbled down the stairs, wincing as a sudden pain shot down his arm. Stealthily, he went home.

Mrs Clark was surprised not to find her husband in bed in the morning. Perhaps he was downstairs feeding the snails. Shockingly, she saw him lying motionless, covered in slime. Suzy and Mark had left a sticky trail. Mr Clark had suffocated but a broken bone in his arm had amazingly mended itself.

Olivia Shillabeer (7)
Hill View Primary School, Bournemouth

THE TIMES WITH MY GRANDMA

Chapter one: Bluebell Wood

We walked around the church cheerfully and I read out all the names on the gravestones, trees and flowerpots, hoping that I would never have to read my grandma's or grandad's name.

Chapter two: Strawberry, Cornish ice cream

Then we strolled to the farm shop and all had Cornish ice cream. Grandma had strawberry, she had pink lips and a pearl-pink moustache, it looked like she had pink lipstick on.

Chapter three: Bubbly Jacuzzi

We were splashing around in a private swimming pool when our legs got really tired and we were worn out, so we jumped into the Jacuzzi for a relax.

Chapter four: Shop 'til we drop

My grandma bought me lots of things and I love them because she bought them for me, but sadly she passed away. Anyway she was a great grandma and she will always be.

Elizabeth Brewer (9)
Hill View Primary School, Bournemouth

A TRUE STORY ABOUT MY GRANDAD

Tuesday 12th of March, 2002 - this is the day that I'm going to tell you about:

My grandad was a milkman but he retired on his birthday. Now he likes to ski a lot.

Years ago when my grandad was a milkman and when he was about twenty-seven he took milk to this lady, she was a really nice woman. Every day she wrote a note saying ring the doorbell, so he rang the doorbell and when the woman opened the door, the house really stank and was really horrible. It was like, you know, when you open a dustbin and it smells really horrible, well that's what it was like.

The lady kept leaving a letter saying, 'Please ring the doorbell'. So he kept ringing, day after day after day. Then one day she asked him to ring again, so he did and she said, 'Could you come inside and have a cup of tea?'
He said, 'Well okay but I'd better be quick.'
So she gave him a cup of tea but the cup had a massive chip in it, then she said, 'Come on, there's something I need to show you.'
They walked into the lounge and lying in there was a dead fox.
My grandad said, 'What's that doing here?'
The lady said that it had just wandered in on its own and died. Grandad asked her why she hadn't put it outside?

The fox was all mouldy and smelly and Grandad said that he wouldn't touch it and the lady would have to call in the RSPCA.

Next time the lady left a note out for Grandad to ring the bell, he just left the milk and carried quickly on.

Maisie Dunning (8)
Hill View Primary School, Bournemouth

THE GIRL WHO TURNED INTO A TOAD

Once upon a time there was a girl called Hollie, she was a pleasant girl. She always told the truth and never lied. Then one day she told a lie and she was so upset she kept on telling more and more lies. She turned into a horrible big toad with spots on her face.

She would never turn back into a person not until someone kissed her fair, soft lips to awaken her - but that never ever happened.

Candie Glascodine (8)
Hill View Primary School, Bournemouth

A GHOSTLY TALE

This story begins on a cold and misty evening in October. A young boy named George had lost his way in the mist coming home from school. He was skipping through the forest on a path he didn't recognise, when he came across an old rusty gate. A cold hand of fear crept around his heart when he realised he was lost.

He walked over and heaved open the heavy iron gates. What he saw took his breath away. A huge, grey, stone castle was towering above him. Silver mist swirled around its many turrets. Creepy gargoyles stared down at him. He crept nervously towards the large oak door. Yet strangely, something felt familiar. A piercing howl filled the cold air and he spun around. Bloodthirsty hounds prowled up and down the wide stone steps. Terrified he ran through the unlocked doors and quickly bolted them with a large slam.

Breathing fast, he looked around the room. Large cobwebs hung from every corner and thick dust covered the floor. A battered staircase twisted upwards. Something drew him forward and he began to climb the stairs as if in a trance. At the top, there was a dark landing hung with several portraits.

He tiptoed forward and reached out to touch a painting of a young boy. Mysteriously his hand glided straight through it. Then he found his whole body being transported into the picture.

He found himself standing in a small room with a tatty old mirror in the corner. He edged forward towards it. Looking into it, he saw a pale reflection of a young boy. The boy was transparent and had dark, sunken eyes. George waved his hand into the mirror and he noticed the boy in the mirror did the same.

George was a ghost.

Alexandra Wigmore (9)
Hill View Primary School, Bournemouth

THE HAUNTED HOUSE

One sunny day, Ash asked his dad if he could take his friend Bruno camping. His dad said yes and they starting packing. Ash ran to tell Bruno that he could go camping with them. They set off with their dog, Fang, and found a nice camping place where they started unpacking.

Bruno ran off quickly to get some firewood. Meanwhile, Ash helped his dad with the sleeping bags. Bruno was picking wood when he looked up and noticed an abandoned house. He rushed back to tell Ash, so then they went to find the house where they slowly opened the creaky door.

Inside they saw a broken door with creaky floorboards and an owl flew over them. They advanced up the stairs and one of the boards on the stairs broke as Bruno trod on it. Ash helped Bruno up and then they noticed a dark room and in the room they found an old, dusty wardrobe. Ash quickly opened the wardrobe door and a skeleton fell out.

Ash and Bruno ran out of the room when they saw some ladders leading to the attic. They advanced up the ladder to look round the room and they spotted a bats' nest.

Suddenly they saw a ghost and rushed back out of the house to the campsite. Ash's dad followed them to the abandoned house and the boys led him to the attic where the bats flew down the stairs and frightened them. When Ash's dad saw the ghost they discovered that it was the dog which had a sheet over it.

Matthew Walker (9)
Hill View Primary School, Bournemouth

STOP THE TEASING!

'We judges will be announcing the girls who have got into the show 'Swish' in five minutes, I repeat five minutes,' yelled the judges.

There was a lot of talented show girls in the group and there were some not quite so talented show girls in their group. But the most talented girl was a girl called Sophie. The bad thing about her was that she liked to tease people.

'The girl chosen for the show 'Swish' is . . . Sophie Wilkinson!'
'*Yippee!* You're a loser Maria Herlin. I got in - not you, ha ha!'
'Sorry, I made a mistake!'
'*What!*'
'The girl chosen for the show 'Swish' is . . . Maria Herlin!'
'Oh my god, I'm in! Yes! This is the best day of my life,' said Maria.

Soon all the people walked out but Maria walked out with her big script.

Over the next few days, Maria was working on her script until she'd learned all the words. Today it was the show and Maria was very nervous but on stage she didn't forget a word.

After the show, Maria was tired, so she went home and tucked herself up in her warm, cosy bed!

So the teasing came to an end and Maria had got her own back on *Sophie Wilkinson!*

Shannon Hamerston (8)
Hill View Primary School, Bournemouth

THE GHOSTLY NIGHTMARES

Sam curled up under the duvet. 'Don't let me have that nightmare again,' he said. He was so frightened he went back to sleep. Suddenly he heard a noise and he woke up again. 'I hope that noise was just my dreamcatcher banging on the window!'

Finally, it was the morning and his mum had promised that he could go to the forest with his cousin Alex.

'Come on Sam!'
When they got in the car Sam was shaking like mad because he'd remembered last night when he'd had those dreams. Alex's mum said the boys could go ahead whilst she stayed behind to get the picnic bag from the car.

Sam always found the forest enchanting and a place where he felt so relaxed but for some reason he felt anxious and the hairs on the back of his head stood up.
'Come on!' shouted Alex. 'I've found a den!'

The boys pulled the bushes to one side and entered the den.
'I can see a pair of red glowing eyes.'
Sam took a step back. 'Let's go! Let's go!' he shouted.
'I'm too scared. Sue help!'
Sue approached from the nearby trees.
'Thank goodness Sue, please take us home!'
Sue was Alex's mum.

When they got home he told his mum all about it. His mum laughed.
'It's nine o'clock and time for bed.'
'Oh Mum, but what if I have a nightmare?'
'Don't be silly, you won't,' said his mum.

Rachel Hunt (8)
Hill View Primary School, Bournemouth

THE MAYOR'S GHOST

In the mysterious woods, far away, Matt, an ordinary eight-year-old boy, found himself lost. He sat down by the largest tree he could see whilst thinking how to get home, until he was distracted by a dragging noise. So Matt carried on walking, getting more and more curious by the minute. But as he got a little further on, the noise came to a halt, but only because Matt had been thrown back by it!

He could only just see it when he got up. He recognised it with a glare, it was the mayor, but how could he be a ghost? It flew past the tree that Matt had left his bag leaning on.

Matt began to chase the ghost from behind, grabbing his bag on the way. Luckily wherever Matt had stopped, he walked in a house feeling tired. Once again, he fell down this time with shock. With a little peer out of the corner of his eye, he saw the real Mayor - which caused him to faint.
'There are two of you!' he screamed. 'You're a clone!'

The mayor decided to sit down and explain everything. Then funnily enough it all went back to normal and Matt went home, living peacefully with his mum and the mayor did also.

But suddenly when they were all sitting eating, the noise reappeared. They all knew it, the ghost had returned to seek revenge and succeeded.

Matthew Hall (8)
Hill View Primary School, Bournemouth

THE MISTREATED SHED

There was a family who lived in a nice house with a lovely garden and a nice big shed. The children did not look after the shed, they threw their bikes and toys into it and always left it very untidy. The shed was very unhappy about this.

One day the family moved and left the poor shed behind, it was in a very sorry state and felt very mistreated.

When the new family moved in and the shed realised there were more children, it decided to get its own back. It knocked over all the bikes and toys and left everything untidy. It encouraged creepy-crawlies to come and live in dark corners and it kept unlocking the door.

The children were very upset and could not understand what was happening. They left the shed tidy but their mum kept telling them off for leaving it in such a mess. All their bikes began to rust as the shed would open the door when it was raining and let everything get wet.

One day as the children were tidying the shed again! They were talking about the strange shed and how they really liked having somewhere to keep all their toys and that one day they would like to decorate it.

The shed listened and realised that these children were different. Slowly the shed began to look after the toys and stopped unlocking the door. It liked the children's company and soon they all became great friends.

Lauren Sansom (8)
Hill View Primary School, Bournemouth

SOMEONE

The door creaked as the spider slid down its web and onto the dust-covered floor.

The sun was going down but my journey was just beginning. I had reached the house and was determined to discover the truth. If this house was haunted, I was going to find out.

I had not even begun to take in my surroundings when I saw a shadow move across the top of the stairs. I was scared but curious so I crept up the stairs and into a room of darkness. The silence was too much to bear but as I was about to leave and return to the world of safety, a noise came from under the unused bed. I tiptoed so as not to make a sound even though it felt as if my heart could wake the dead.

I crept down, tilted my head, lifted the duvet and the mice scuttled past. I knelt down to regain my composure and I felt a cold breath on the back of my neck. Someone was breathing behind me but as I turned it stopped. The shadow had moved, it was now inside the wardrobe which was so old that I could see through the cracked doors. It had stopped moving - it was waiting for me.

I was scared but I had to see it. My hand shook as I reached for the handle. The door creaked but suddenly I was pulled in. I saw it and knew that I would never escape.

Danielle-Elyse Fordham (9)
Hill View Primary School, Bournemouth

AT BEDTIME

It was bedtime for a little girl, her name is Sophie, she is five. Sophie always has nightmares and dreams at bedtime.

That night she had a nightmare, she was in a school and loads of things were chasing her and then they caught her. Sophie thought that they were going to hurt her but then all of the things were her friends.

Sophie said, 'Hello, what are you doing?'
'Nothing!' came the reply.

Sophie woke up in the morning and said, 'That dream I had last night was strange.'

Louise Goral (9)
Hill View Primary School, Bournemouth

CREEPY CASTLE IN THE NIGHT

In Oak village there were two boys named Tom and Sam.

Tom and Sam wanted to find monsters and ghosts so that people would believe that they existed. They wanted to go into the woods but their parents wouldn't let them because it was dangerous.

At midnight they crept out of bed, they got their camera with a special ghost lens, notebook and video camera then they silently ran out of the house into the woods. The woods were very scary, creepy and spooky because the trees looked like monsters in the dark. They shone the torchlight on the ground and saw weird-looking footprints they followed them to a spooky castle.

They looked at the door, it was very big. It opened with a creak, they went inside, they heard groans and growls. They investigated the castle and all they could find were cobwebs, spiders and creepy-crawlies.

Suddenly lightning flashed through the window, they heard thunder crashing like rocks falling from the cliffs. They went into the hall. Tom saw a ghost and took a photo of it. Sam described what it looked like in the notebook, they heard something coming down the stairs. It was a big, scary monster. They hid away so that it wouldn't find them. Sam filmed it on the video camera then they broke a window to get free and ran back to the village to their parents to show them that monsters really exist.

Wesley Jameson (9)
Hill View Primary School, Bournemouth

THE EXPLORER CAT

Slam! I was in the boot of my family's car. I was off to the beach miaaaaow! It was too hot and I was scared, it was very dark in here. I was very thirsty and I wondered when I would get out.

The car suddenly stopped with a massive jolt. Oops! I was off my feet and on to the floor. To my amazement we had broken down but my family didn't know I was there. I had been nosy and wanted to see what was in the picnic hamper and the lady of the house had shut the boot of the big black car before I'd had time to leap out to safety. She had been busy with the two boys, getting them in the car for their trip.

My family got out, I think they were admiring the wheels, I frantically scratched, hoping they would hear me. They opened the boot and I hopped out. I was panting like a dog who had just run for a stick. *'Gripper!'* They all yelled. I hopped back into the boot in fright.

The man of the house called the breakdown truck. The lady picked me up and put me in the truck. *Vroom! Vroom!* The great big truck started. I was high up in the cab and could see all around me, the houses and trees whizzed by. There were lots of cars and great big lorries, *I don't think I like the world out here much.*

At last we were home, the man of the house carried me in and gave me a bowl of water. The family didn't go to the beach that day, they stayed home to look after me and see if I was all right. After a drink, I curled up on the sofa and fell straight to sleep.

The next day the family decided to go back to the beach as their big black car had been mended - this time I wasn't so nosy!

Luke Jackson (8)
Hill View Primary School, Bournemouth

THE SPOOKY GOINGS ON AT MICHAEL'S MANOR

Dad came back from work late. He called Mum in, coughed slightly, so I knew he was going to say something important, and announced, 'My company's relocating to Kent. They've rented us a manor house.'

When I first saw the manor it looked haunted. Inside it was worse. The doors creaked, the banister was dusty and the rooms had cobwebs.

That night, when I fell asleep, I dreamt about a ghost searching for a blood-red ruby ring. I woke up and decided on going downstairs to have a glass of water. When I got downstairs the clock chimed midnight, and out of nowhere came the ghost I had dreamt about.
'Hello there, what brings you down here at this time of night?' asked the ghost, and very politely in my opinion.
'I had a dream about a ghost just like you, he was searching for a ring,' I replied.
'You know about the ring, can you help me look for it?' he asked.
'Yes, let's try my room,' I suggested.

We searched every nook and cranny. Eventually I managed to wrench up a floorboard and there it was, sitting there so elegantly as if it had been waiting for us. Magically it levitated up to the ghost.
'Thank you, now my spirit may rest in peace,' he said, and vanished in a puff of smoke.

A year later we've bought a house and Dad still comes home late from work.

Andrew Sheppard (9)
Hill View Primary School, Bournemouth

PLAYSTATION MANIAC

It was a dark night down Crystal Lane. The trees swayed in the breeze and the moon lit up the street. No one expected something strange to happen. Suddenly the moon disappeared behind a cloud. A man, old, wrinkled and about two metres tall, appeared with a pop. He looked around, then ran off to No 4 and placed a letter on the 'welcome' mat, then, without a warning, disappeared.

Anne woke with a start. She couldn't remember the dream she'd been having but it had been a good one. She pulled on her dressing gown, and slumped downstairs. She was a tall, pale-skinned girl with long, curly, ginger locks and bright blue eyes that sparkled like stars and bursting with life. Her brother, Ryan, was already eating breakfast. Ryan was Anne's twin brother, he had short, blonde hair and emerald-green eyes.
'Get the post Anne,' Ryan said as soon as she came in.
'Fine,' said Anne, 'leave the hard work to me!'

She scowled at her brother and stalked off. The letter was addressed to her and her brother. *Strange,* she thought, *we never get letters!* She padded softly back.
'What's that?' Ryan asked with a mouthful of cornflakes.
'Hum, it's a snake, what does it look like? It's a letter!' shouted Anne.
'I only asked,' replied Ryan.
Anne opened the letter, big mistake!

Darkness fell all around them. Suddenly they looked up and saw an enormous, dark, angry *giant!*
'We're in the PlayStation!' gasped Ryan.

Lydia Gyngell (10)
Hill View Primary School, Bournemouth

THE BOX

'Sonny Jim! Come give your grandad a hug.'

Robbie's grandfather was 63 years old. He had short grey hair and thick ugly glasses.

'Hi Grandad.' Robbie was 12 years old. He was short and slim. He had brown hair, though nobody ever saw it as he was always wearing his cap. He was on half-term and had to stay round his grandad's house as his mum was working.

'Now, you'll never guess what fun stuff we'll be doing today?'

'I don't know Grandad, please tell me?'

'We'll be cleaning out my loft!'

Robbie's eyes rolled. 'I'm so . . . excited.'

'Great! There's not a moment to lose.'

When they reached the loft, Robbie raced inside, hoping to get it over and done with.

'You start over there.'

Robbie walked over. As he rummaged through the pile of socks, he heard as noise. He ignored it and carried on. As he did, he found a small, old, dusty box. 'Grandad, what's this box for?' Robbie asked, wiping off the dust.

'Ah, I was sold that in Egypt. Said to be cursed. Very valuable though. Guy called Mr Jones, who was fantastic at everything, really wanted this. But fifty years on he still hasn't got it. It's still mine.'

'But not for long.' Slowly a dark figure entered the room.

'Mr Jones!'

'Give me the box little boy or I'll shoot you!'

'Give him the box Robbie.'

Robbie cautiously handed over the box. Mr Jones smiled. However, Mr Jenkins gave a sly smile back as he opened the box.

Philip Baker (11)
Hill View Primary School, Bournemouth

THE NOT SO FAMOUS FOUR

Gemma pushed her way through the crowd on the school bus. As she stepped out a cool breeze swept past her bony cheeks. As not to be late, she rushed along the street to the post office to meet her brothers and sister and get into her warm, cosy house on the corner of a narrow road. As she rushed across the pavement her feet crunched in the snow. She reached the post office and standing there shivering were her two brothers, Josh and Dan, and her sister, Samantha. Quickly they ran home to get in the warm.

Inside the house you could get a lovely view of the sea. Now, their mother and father were the kindest people you could meet. They offered food and drink and gave sweets to children.

Once the children were inside the house and were having a hot drink and biscuits in front of the TV, they discussed their next adventure. They were thinking about staying there as there was going to be some quite bad weather, but Dan adored going on adventures and he was trying to persuade everyone to go on their boat to an island. They made a deal that if the weather was good they would go to the island, if not they would stay at home.

They woke with a start the next day and saw the sun and started packing. They set sail. All of a sudden rain started to pour and lightning flew down.

Emily Curtis-Bennett (10)
Hill View Primary School, Bournemouth

THE GHOST OF NEW YEAR'S EVE

On the Friday of New Year's Eve a mysterious ghost appeared when Big Ben struck 12 o'clock. It was a ghost which looked like it was half lion and half eagle. When people saw the ghost their bottom jaw dropped. The people of London were gobsmacked at the awesome sight of this tremendously big ghost gliding through the air.

As the gigantic ghost passed over the moon you could see the moon through the body of the ghost. Then the clock struck 1 o'clock and the enormous ghost swooped inside Big Ben. By now the people on the streets had disappeared and all the commotion on the streets had cleared, and the streets were bare.

The next day the streets were flooded again. The day after that a boy called Tom went to see if he could discover where the ghost's home was in Big Ben. Tom found the ghost inside the bell of the clock and instead of the ghost being scary and furious, it was crying and weeping. Then a sad but bellowing voice sniffed, 'When I go out for a fly trying to find a friend, everyone runs away. I am getting too lonely.'
Tom replied in a soft voice, 'It's because you look scary, but I'll be your friend.'

Gareth Jenkins (10)
Hill View Primary School, Bournemouth

PATRICK ROBERTS AND THE TEMPLE OF DOOM

One day there was a person called Patrick Roberts. He had a dad but his mum was dead. She died a long time ago.

They had a quest to solve that looked really good. Patrick and Matthew wanted to do it, so they did. They left in a helium balloon at the United States airfield.

There was a slight problem, when they were in the air a bomb hit the side of the balloon and in the balloon there was a robber, so Patrick held him up while Matthew stabbed him with a knife. The robber fell straight into a hole. They stopped the balloon from crashing.

Patrick Roberts and Matthew Bruno then got into a plane. They drove off and let the balloon fly away. While they were in the aeroplane, there were two more about fifty metres away, so Patrick told Matthew to start firing at them and he got both of them. They got up to a ridge and landed with quite a safe landing.

They got out and a spear started to fly straight past them and landed right by Patrick's foot, near his big toe. Patrick took a dagger which was by his foot and it was pretty hard to get out of the ground. Matthew Bruno and Patrick carried on walking to where they had to go. They got there just in time before the ruby diamond was gone. Patrick had to go through cutting blades. After he got through he said he had to go over the unusable steps.

Patrick Roberts (9)
Hill View Primary School, Bournemouth

THE MAN IN BLACK

One scary, spooky night, when a full moon was out, a group of girls were having a party. Just as they were going to turn the music down, they heard a knock on the door. As they opened the door there was a man standing there in black. He had a hand rifle in his hand. They slammed the door shut and rang the police, but by the time the police got there the man had gone. Well, that's what they thought but really he was just round the corner.

They thought they would never see him again till one cold night there was a knock at the door. They had forgotten about the man with the gun, but when they opened the door and saw the man they remembered him. He asked if he could come in. They slammed the door shut and rang the police.

This time the police were there in one second flat and they caught him.

Zachary Bryan (10)
Hill View Primary School, Bournemouth

THE TALKING DOG

A long time ago there was a talking dog who lived by itself in a flat. He lived on his own because his owner, who he loved, went to prison for drug dealing. The talking dog, called Punk, loved his owner so much he was making a plan to get him out of prison.

He had it - he got up and ran as fast as a cheetah towards the prison next to the Millennium Stadium. He ran in the prison and luckily the policemen were nowhere in sight. Punk chewed his way through the bars. When there was a big enough space to get through, Punk and his owner ran out.

The policemen ran out chasing them, so they ran into the Millennium Stadium and hid in the middle of the fans at the game when Bournemouth won 5-2 against Lincoln. Punk and his owner, Josh, jumped on the back of the getaway (or players' bus) home, but what would happened when they were all over the TV and newspaper?

Later that night they watched the 10 o'clock news and realised they were on TV, so they packed their stuff and ran away to Liverpool. They had to go through the sewers to get there unseen. When they came out they came up next to some policemen and they were both thrown back in prison.

Stuart Lane (10)
Hill View Primary School, Bournemouth

THE TIGERS AND THE HUNTERS

In the humid jungle a group of tigers were hiding in the long green grass waiting for their prey to arrive.

Suddenly a tiger leapt out and dug its teeth into the boar's neck. The boar screamed and slowly weakened and in under a minute it was dead. The group ran towards the meat.

Suddenly the dominant male roared and every tiger stopped and stared at him. Then he said, 'I can hear a jeep, go and hide really well.'
So all the tigers went a mile away and found a new home, while the dominant male stayed behind to make sure everything and everyone had vanished. The jeep burst through the jungle into the old home of the group and the dominant male ran, but he also covered his tracks. He caught up with the group and agreed to stay in his new home.

Two weeks later the hunters were back. This time they were successful and killed two tigers, one was the dominant male's mate. This made him furious and he ran after the hunters. He pounced on the jeep and bit the driver's head off and suffocated the other man by grabbing his throat with his teeth. He took the men to his new home and the group feasted on them.

They then lived happily ever after.

Amy Rickman (9)
Hill View Primary School, Bournemouth

THE INCREDIBLE HULK

David Banner was trying to look for a serum to stop him turning into the Incredible Hulk. The reason why he didn't want to turn into the Hulk is because he broke things. But, he does save people's lives.

David Banner only turns into the Hulk when he is mad or angry. For example, he saved a few people's lives by catching a helicopter falling from the sky. He was fuming when he heard about the bank robbery. His eyes bulged out like two tortoise shells, his muscles began to bulge, his knuckles were ready to smash and his jaw was ready to snap. He pulled his car door open and just managed to get in, but he burst all the tyres, and the doors and roof fell off. He ran all the way to the bank.

The Hulk saw the bank robbers and caught up with them. He sprang into action and held two of the robbers while the other robbers backed off. The Hulk threw the two robbers, who he had tightly in his hands. They went right over a bridge and into the water. He saved the safe from being stolen. There was 300 million dollars in the safe.

The people on the news said they saw a massive green giant with big bulky muscles and green fuzzy hair. The people are still trying to look for the Hulk, but they did not know that the Hulk is a normal person.

David Banner is still looking for a cure.

Charles R Gilbey (9)
Hill View Primary School, Bournemouth

DE HAVILLAND

De Havilland planes were made near us in Southampton during the Second World War. De Havilland made lots of planes like the Dragon, the Moth which was a bi-plane, the Mosquito and the Comet. They made planes for both racing and fighting around the time of the war. A lot of their planes were made of wood or plywood.

I have seen a De Havilland Vampire in the Aviation Museum in Bournemouth's Hurn Airport. Even though it is more modern, it is still made of plywood. The plane in the museum is fully working and can actually fly.

Most De Havillands are twin-engined. I liked twin-engined planes as they were very fast and a nice shape. Two men sat in a Comet, one man sat in a Moth and two in a Mosquito. There were almost eight thousand Mosquitoes made in England, Canada and Australia because it was such a successful plane. At the beginning of the war it was the fastest plane in the sky.

The Comet was built for the 1934 England to Australia air race which it won. The Comet still flies in air shows today. In the Aviation Museum they have an old photograph of the Comet being restored.

I have made an Airfix model of a Comet. Its number is thirty-four and it is bright red.

One day I would like to help build or restore a De Havilland plane, and I would love to fly the Comet.

Daniel Coe Vissenga (9)
Hill View Primary School, Bournemouth

THE WOOD OF ADVENTURES

Once upon a time there was a girl called Emily and a boy called George. Emily was seven and George was nine. They had just moved to a cottage in the countryside with their mum and dad and their dog called Inker.

One day their mother asked Emily and George to go and pick some mushrooms from the wood, which was very lucky indeed because the wood was very near to them.

When they got there and saw the huge juicy mushrooms, they were so eager to take a bite that they didn't remember to check if they were the right sort. As soon as they bit into them they expanded in their mouths and they felt fizzy and most peculiar.

Suddenly they heard something under the ground but no, it wasn't an animal noise, because they could understand it. What was it? A squirrel passed by, but what a shock it got when it heard them speaking a language it could understand. You see, the mushrooms were magic ones and if you ate one you could talk to animals and understand them.

Suddenly they heard a strange noise. It was a hedgehog and she looked very upset. They went over to see what was wrong. At first she seemed frightened but after they explained to her why they could talk, she told them she had lost all her five babies. The two children said they would help.

They walked through the bushes and along the path until Emily looked under a bush and found three of the little hedgehogs cuddled up together. They were very pleased to see their mother again.

They started to walk a bit further and then George found the other ones in a big patch of grass and she was so happy that she couldn't think of a word to say and was crying for joy. She thanked the children and gave them a beautiful leaf that was extremely precious to them because it had been passed down for many generations.

After, they walked back merrily and they lived happily ever after.

Elizabeth Heygate-Browne (9)
Hill View Primary School, Bournemouth

THE ADVENTURES OF THE FIVE DRAGONS

A long time ago there lived five brave baby dragons who got separated from their parents when an evil wizard captured their parents and took them away to his dungeon. The baby dragons managed to escape the wizard.

They set off on an adventure to find someone to help them to rescue their parents.

The baby dragons were all different colours - Ben was blue and he was fearless, Coco was yellow and he had a funny sense of humour, Inky was orange and he was the imaginative one, Flame was very red and he was the brainy one, and then there was Cookie, he was green and he was always hungry.

Who could they ask to help them? The only people they could think of were the strange creatures that lived on the Island of Fear. The creatures were human-sized frogs that walked on two legs and had four arms that they used to row their fine boats. The baby dragons knew about the frogs because their father told them stories about the brave frogs. But on the same island there lived a huge creature-like beast, that was half man, half lizard, that was why it was called Fear Island.

The baby dragons made their way to Fear Island, they found the frogs and they asked them for their help to rescue their parents. The frogs said they would help the baby dragons but first they must kill the lizard.

The frogs and the baby dragons went to the lizard's castle when they got there luck was on all their side, because the wizard was there with the baby dragons' parents. The frogs rescued the dragons by leaping up to let them out of the cage they were kept in and the baby dragons, and the frogs knocked the castle to the ground.

The lizard and wizard were never to be seen again.

Jack Walden (8)
Hill View Primary School, Bournemouth

A DAY IN THE LIFE OF A TABBY CAT

Oh no! Little sticky hands are coming my way. Do you mind? Watch my tail. I managed to escape through the hole in the door. Life saver that is!

Next door's cat again. She hissed at me furiously. I walked off swaying my tail from side to side, showing off as she glared at me and I started licking my paws. Oh look, it's the humans coming.

I jumped up as she stroked my shiny fur and I proudly purred in her ear. I was just about to settle down when a dog decided to explore our garden. 'Hiss!' I certainly made sure it didn't come back again.

Suddenly I spotted a great big, juicy spider with my eyes. I started chasing it around the garden squashing it under my paws. Then a human bellowed, 'Pebbles, leave the spider alone.'

I plodded up the stairs onto the comfy bed and started to close my eyes for a long sleep. Yawn! Peace at last . . .

Emma Humphrey (11)
Holbury Junior School, Southampton

A DAY IN THE LIFE OF A RADIATOR

It was cold outside - winter had come around again. People around me were shivering but I was alright. My eyes peered around the room, the light was switched off and I was alone once more. A shiver ran down my spine. It had started to snow. I can go from hot to cold in a matter of seconds, I really gets on my nerves.

I'm getting old and I think they are going to replace me. My time is nearly done. My tummy rumbled, it really hurts. I think I'm coming down with something, maybe pneumonia. I'm not surprised with all this cold.

Oh look, here is someone, no . . . no what are you doing? He is taking me away. What did I tell you? My time is done. I better make the most of daylight while I can. You know what this means, I will be crushed . . . . squashed even. Goodbye, sweet world, goodbye.

Bethany Keen (11)
Holbury Junior School, Southampton

A DAY IN THE LIFE OF A BOXER DOG

Oh no! Big, tall human coming my way! Sticky hands grabbing me and shoving me off the large, comfy sofa.

Next door's cat again, I'm ready to pounce . . . *crash!* I'm nearly there, getting closer, you just wait until next time!

Yay! The postman's here, I'm ready to growl! I go outside, lying on my back, trying to catch flies and dragonflies.

Oh no, not again! Humans I'm talking about . . . hang on a minute I can smell lamb and chicken and the freshness of the cold water. It's my breakfast coming. Mmm . . . I feel like a walk now because it's 7.30am, not that early.

Woof! Woof! The cat's outside again. I spotted, in the corner of my eye while watching the cat walking along the fence, a daddy-long-legs . . . *snap!* That was lovely.
'Cassie, stop messing about.'

Gradually I plodded to the sofa and climbed on it. I yawned! Aah, peace at last.

Lauren Burrow (11)
Holbury Junior School, Southampton

A DAY IN THE LIFE OF A TESCO'S TROLLEY

Yawn! Oh for goodness sake, I'm not ready to wake up yet. Leave me alone . . . ouch! Mind the chains mate! I know it's a good idea to lock us up an' all, but please go easy on us, we work our wheels off all day every day.

Oh no. Stroppy teenager at eight o'clock. Looks like I'm in for a tough time; pushed and shoved violently through the familiar aisles of goods that these humans exchange for shiny paper and gold coins. I see all this time and time again. I'm the thing that they use to pile up the goods in.

Finally back to the place where I'm supposed to go until somebody else comes to choose me. Hang on; we're going the wrong way! Turn me round mate! Please, not the road, no, please don't push me in the river, please, help!

This is the worst day of my life. Definitely. It can't get any worse. *Crash!* Okay, maybe it can. This rain is going to get my wheels in a spin for sure. Goodness knows where I'll end up when I get out of this river. Yuk; I'm covered in sewage! I'm as foul as a public toilet.

A powerful current coming in from the south. I'm in trouble now. I don't think I'll ever see Tesco's again. This is not my day. Help! *Snap . . . crash . . . bang . . .*

Oh, my head. What happened? The river, the stroppy teenager. Everything's flooding back to me. Speaking of flooding, looks like that strong current's got the worst of me. I was thrown into the air by such a force that I collided with a nearby tree and then fell with a thump onto the ground, followed by a shower of leaves. From then on, everything went black.

I suppose I'd better get back, although I'm as exhausted as a car exhaust. Imagine being a car exhaust, puffing out all those deadly fumes. Oh look, here comes the trolley guard.
'Where have you been?' he grumbled roughly.

I was taken back and locked up along with all the other trolleys.

I hope by reading this you ignorant humans will understand how hard a trolley's life is. That goes for you too, trolley guard. Maybe you'll go more easy on the chains next time.

Chloe Smith (11)
Holbury Junior School, Southampton

A DAY IN THE LIFE OF A DESIGNER HAT

Oh, don't even go there! What makes you think you can afford me, I'm a designer. I proudly turned my mauve brim edging as I sat above those *non-designers*.

A small-sized human approached me. Her blonde hair and her huge nit. *Her huge nit?* What am I doing. I am a Jasper Conran! I don't deserve this treatment. I stuck out my J label.

Anyway, it was huge, brown, vicious and blood-sucking. Deadlier than ever. I found myself in such relief to be taken away and cleaned up. I almost frayed!

Where am I? In this thick, bluey hole. It's not perfect but it beats the nit zone!

Kyla Armstrong (11)
Holbury Junior School, Southampton

A DAY IN THE LIFE OF . . .

I woke up in a glistening, silky bed and slowly walked away from it. As soon as I had exited my comfy house, I jogged along to my huge, lumpy climbing tree where my ancient bug trap lay as still as a log.

As I climbed up to my trap, a colourful bird flew past me and nearly knocked me off of all my eight legs. As I had just got my grip back, I could just see out into the distance, a small bug was caught in the sticky trap.

I started trotting along the branch as jolly as a jolly postman. As soon as I got to my trap I heard a strange noise coming from the distance. Oh no! It's my arch rival, the hawk eagle. It's heading straight towards me!

It crashed straight into me, hurtling away from the tree. I tried shooting some silk to a branch and wrapping it around the big branch but it wouldn't reach! I knew now that I was going to fall to my death!

Shane Wynn (11)
Holbury Junior School, Southampton

LEAF

I am high in the sky, swaying in the breeze, holding onto my stick as hard as I can. When the light bulb shines brightly on me, I like to show off my beautiful, green, shiny skin, trying to be the best of the pack.

When the light bulb is switched off this wet stuff falls from the sky and onto my body. I quite like it, it makes my skin much more shiny.

One day, my skin turned brown and orange and I fell to the ground as softly as could be.

A few weeks later . . . cold, wet powder flew to the ground, covering me. 'Help, I can't move!' Ow, for tree's sake! I'm cold, thirsty and annoyed.

Finally I'm free. I can't remember what heat feels like. I'm climbing up the tower but I keep slipping down. I give up I'm useless. I might as well be free, free to roam the planet, free to go anywhere I want. I miss the good life.

Sam Read (11)
Holbury Junior School, Southampton

A DAY IN THE LIFE OF A DOLPHIN

I started making noises for attention. Where is everybody? I wanted to play! I glided up to the crowd of people, what were they all staring at? Suddenly my dinner came flying through the air. Oh yummy! I caught it in my mouth - delicious!

Afterwards I called to my friends and then we played a game of tag. I dived to the bottom of the sea, rubbing my back against the sand. The sun was beaming and my rubbery skin was getting warmer and warmer. I looked up at the clear blue sky, then spouted out water and it went over my back, nice and cold!

Ellisha Nemec (10)
Holbury Junior School, Southampton

A DAY IN THE LIFE OF A DICTIONARY

'Ow! Slow down Mary - and you Jake - I hope you remember what independence means: an action or thought with no co-operation or help from another someone or something else.

What a miserable day, aww, what's that? Ooorrr just unfold my arm. Ouch! There, that's better, I hate it when that happens. Aaah. It's so annoying.'
'Well you're not the only one, it's our duty.'
'Do what? Suffer pain and agony just to mark someone's place in me or being thrown on the floor, disrespected, ruined and dumped here! Right here. Just anywhere, they don't care. It's just an excuse to pretend they're working.'

'If you had listened to what I was saying and not interrupted me . . . anyway what sort of influence on the rest of the books do you show slumping around moaning?'
'I have my reasons, trust me.'
'Yeah whatever, you were not meant to be! You should be a tramp, living off trash and see how thankful you'd be then.'
'Oh come on, oh just forget it I didn't mean it like that.'
I looked towards the ceiling soothing my bent arms then to my utter surprise . . . errrr, that's disgusting. Oh I'm all wet - yuck! Who dribbled? Rip, tear, break, crack, *no! Never!* Please. That's 11 down 1139 to go.

Hannah Duffy (11)
Holbury Junior School, Southampton

A Day In The Life Of A Hamster

Yawn! One eye opens then another. I crawl out of my cubbyhole, hoping that breakfast is ready. I walk across the freezing floor of my house into my dining room. I see sunflower seeds and carrots. I start to tuck into a carrot, nibbling the outside of the carrot first.

It must be nine o'clock because X-Change is on. Five past nine, exercise time. Up five tubes, down two tubes, across one tube, there, we are here, in my exercise room. I have got a wheel, maze and a tunnel. I have great fun in here!

I have just come out of the maze. Two hours is the longest I have lasted in my whole life. Back down to the dining room to have a nice long drink.

Now I am going to go and tuck myself in bed and go to sleep. Night.

Sarah Babey (11)
Holbury Junior School, Southampton

A DAY IN THE LIFE OF JAMES BEATTIE'S T-SHIRT

Some people say I'm extremely popular with my two striped colours. It all began when I felt my body being stitched together, first my arms then my body, as if I was a jigsaw puzzle. Then suddenly the number nine was permanently attached to my back, by a *hot* branding iron, which I could feel sizzling rapidly. I found myself in a smelly room filled with impostors copying my style like looking into a mirror. Someone or something grabbed me and shoved a shiny piece of plastic down both of my silky arms.

The next thing I knew there were lots and lots of humans cheering and screaming at me. I was so nervous I started fraying as I began to play. I got swung around many times which first made me feel useless but then in a way special. I heard something very loud and in no time I was back in the smelly and disgusting room.

I was then quickly thrown into a large mouth, which was filled with boiling hot water. I started getting more and more dizzy by the second as it tumbled me over and over. When I came out I felt refreshed as if I had been born over again.

I was then squeezed between a gigantic piece of metal and a massive piece of wood. The time flew by and at the end of the season many famous people held me, most of the impostors' owners. I was put with a loving family that would look at me all the time as if I was a painting done by Van Gogh in a museum.

Becky House (11)
Holbury Junior School, Southampton

A DAY IN THE LIFE OF A CO-OP BAG

As I woke up, I could feel something heavy inside me. Then a human carried me away. 'Help me!' I cried. I was leaving my mum for sure. After a while the human dropped me. I could see big wooden planks opening and closing. Then a young human emptied me.

Afterwards the human put me in a weird hole with a long plank in front. After a while a large human picked me up and put me on a hard floor. Suddenly a gust of wind blew me away. I didn't know where I was going to end up. I could see a flying object coming towards me. 'Someone save me please,' I shouted. It was getting closer and closer. I couldn't do anything but keep on floating. Then I fell into a large container. It stank like a skunk on a bad day! Then a mechanical creature picked the container up and ate all the rubbish. It took ages before the creature stopped. Then it tipped me into a place I'd never been to before.

I thought I was in Heaven but it couldn't be because heaven has angels and golden gates but this place had rubbish and mouldy apples. I didn't know where I was. 'Please help me, I'm stranded I don't know where I am,' I cried out. I was going to die. I was stranded and no one was going to help me. Other cans and plastic bags were crying out, 'Help me.' I hate being a Co-Op bag.

Sam Goodchild (11)
Holbury Junior School, Southampton

A DAY IN THE LIFE OF A PENCIL CASE

I lay there sunbathing - it was raining though. Those annoying humans kept digging their nails into my spine it was really aggravating. They kept taking things out of me - my vital organs. My mouth kept going up and down like someone in a dentist's chair - it made me so stressed - I was in a right mood.

My delicate cover got torn as a human began throwing me around. I began to cry. They were breaking my bones, it hurt. My skin began to peel off and I was suffering. Then suddenly it all went black and I ended up in Heaven!

Oh it was lovely. There were all sorts of everything I'd ever dreamed of, it was the best day of my life. It smelt like sharpenings, it was the new Lynx deodorant - sharpener flavour. This truly was Heaven.

I saw my grandma and my uncle and auntie, and there was my great, great, great grandad. I began to cry again as they all rolled their way over to me and they began to hug and kiss me on my bright blue cheeks. Disgusting or what.

Liam Smith (11)
Holbury Junior School, Southampton

A DAY IN THE LIFE OF A BEE

I flew out of home on a hot summer's day in my furry coat. I may be dangerous, I may not be dangerous. Just in front of me is a monster with two eyes and no wings.

I landed on a pretty flower and rubbed the seeds on my fur. Just then a pointy thing started to rub my fur, I started to giggle. I rolled on my back but the thing still rubbed me.

I started to move my legs and open my wings. The monster ran away. At last he's gone I can fly away. Tower to tower, then back home. This is my day.

At home my friends and me have to make food for a monster to take and eat.

Todd Lloyd (11)
Holbury Junior School, Southampton

A Day In The Life Of A Rabbit

I'm a cute, loveable, playful thing as cuddly as can be. I laze around in the sun all day and run about my bar wired cage. I clean my fluffy, soft fur so I can be as clean as I can be every day.

I like to drink from my water bottle which hangs on my window sill but I don't know why my food bowl says *Dog*. I'm not a dog, just a small, clever thing.

Jumping around is fun, my friend the hamster says I'm hyper. I like to eat grass, hay, apples, mints and carrots but I'm not a horse.

I like sneaking around and chewing wires joined to my mum's TV. Rat and mouse say we're the same because we like to chew wires, but I'm not.

I'm a cute, cuddly, playful, clever, wire-eating rabbit.

Katie Knight (11)
Holbury Junior School, Southampton

A Day In The Life Of A Football

When I was playing, I was getting very hurt. I could see the place where I was going to land. There were a load of other people looking at me, I was exhausted. I heard loads of screaming and roaring all around me.

My head was swirling round and round like a spinning top spinning on its bottom. My feet were on the ground, I was about to be kicked up the bum. 'Ouch!' I shouted. No one heard me but I did not mind, as a matter of fact, I didn't care much, but it hurt a lot. I did not care because it happened all the time.

Richard Wells (11)
Holbury Junior School, Southampton

A DAY IN THE LIFE OF A BUNNY RABBIT

9am
I lay on my bed curled up as my fur coat bristled against my face. As I slept, in my dream I saw lots of treats like chocolate. *Mmm my favourite.* In my dream I saw lots of chocolate treats.

Two hands picked me up and put me on her lap and started to squeeze me really tight. I may look cute but I'm not, so I do what I please. Whoops, I bit the person. Oh well I will just be in my little house.

10am
Bored stiff, I went to explore. Someone picked me up just as I was about to wee. I did tell you I needed to wee.
Back in my house I went to sleep and started the day all over again.

Victoria Woolley (11)
Holbury Junior School, Southampton

A DAY IN THE LIFE OF A FOOTBALL

When I am playing I get worn out. I can see loads of people. There are loads of people jumping up and down, when I land in a certain place. Then I get pushed out and back in the middle.

I get tired and thirsty, I get flatter. At a certain time I get picked up and rested for about fifteen minutes. Then I get hurt again.

I get used about ten times a week. When someone scores three goals they can take me home.

Dayle Andrews (11)
Holbury Junior School, Southampton

A DAY IN THE LIFE OF A SNAKE

I lay there licking my lips as my prey looked tasty.

Afterwards I went back to my baby, who was asleep in its leafy cot. I might live in the grass or up the trees or in the water. I'm very smooth and big, even though I'm a bit slow. I still poison people with my poisonous bite.

I sometimes swim in the water and I have a very scaly body. I can slither around in the grass too. I get myself dry with my bushy towel. I'm so thick and really very long. My fangs are very vicious and really, really sharp to bite and catch my prey when I'm hungry.

Joshua McPhee (11)
Holbury Junior School, Southampton

144

A DAY IN THE LIFE OF A RING

My friend and me sat sparkling in the sun.
'Ow that hurt me,' I said, rubbing next to my mate, who was a bit older than me.

I used to have a best friend but a posh lady took her away and put her on a little girl. Well, she was small, my best mate.

'Stop, stop, don't touch me. I still want to be clean. Get your human fleas off me.'

I like to ride on my owner because everyone looks and stares at my gorgeous look. My worst enemy is the toe ring, it looks up at me with its evil eyes.

Tara Parry (11)
Holbury Junior School, Southampton

A DAY IN THE LIFE OF A RABBIT

As I sat there in the corner of my home, I started to nibble a bit of the cage to try and break free. But as I tried to get out, my white, fluffy hair got in the way.

Then it was dinner time. I got my favourite food. I don't know what it was but the colour was orange.

Rhianon Jones (11)
Holbury Junior School, Southampton

A DAY IN THE LIFE OF A CAR

People think I'm scary as my eyes glare and people ride me. I only bond with rich people. Famous people adore my delicate skin of shining armour. My tummy rumbles when I'm thirsty.

Jamie Hooper (11)
Holbury Junior School, Southampton

A DAY IN THE LIFE OF A CAR

People like to lay on me because I am hot. Of course I like to race a lot and I win sometimes.

My owner gets a lot of money which is how we afford me and fill me up. When I am ready to go hear me roar.

Cadan Emsley (11)
Holbury Junior School, Southampton

A DAY IN THE LIFE OF A DOG

I sat down on a bed licking my paws then my owner tickled my belly and cuddled me. I went in the garden and lay down under the sun and fell into a deep dream. Then I was getting hot, too hot, so I moved into the shade and fell asleep then ate dinner.

David Burn (11)
Holbury Junior School, Southampton

A DAY IN THE LIFE OF A ROCK

I am a solid, I get thrown and kicked and crushed. I have millions of friends, we get broken and smashed. I am round like a circle. I'm hard and soft and big and sometimes small, my colour is grey. All of my friends die and one day so will I. We get reborn when we get killed. We normally die of all different reasons, getting stamped on, getting crushed. It's just not the life for me or you.

We are always made as a solid. Luckily, we're not born like plastic or something weaker so I'm lucky.

Stuart Taylor (11)
Holbury Junior School, Southampton

A DAY IN THE LIFE OF A HAMSTER

9pm - Wake up.
9.05pm - I scurry across the sawdust.
9.10pm - Yum, food time, nuts again, my favourite.
9.30pm - A big monster with sharp claws comes towards my cage.
10pm - Ouch, I am put in a strange, round cage.
11pm - Yes, back in my usual place!
11.05pm - Someone has messed up my sawdust. Damn!
11.30pm - Time for climbing through those tubes.
12am - I think I'm going to get a drink, I'm dead thirsty.
12.30am - Prepare for a nap.
1am - Nap time! Yes!

Kimberley Longman (11)
Holbury Junior School, Southampton

A DAY IN THE LIFE OF A STONE

I am a stone, I get smashed into billions of particles because of people throwing me everywhere. I sit nearly all day and all night thinking, *if only I was someone else.*

Ouch! Someone's just kicked my backside, argh it's now throbbing like a hammer being slammed down on a thumb. Shriek! I'm being thrown in the air and now I'm flying, whoah! I'm now landing - ouch! My back, I think it's - argh I've smashed into millions and billions of particles and now I've broken off my arm, my leg and my back and oh, I want to be a car instead of a horrible, annoying, moaning stone. Roll on when I die.

Ashley Lewis (11)
Holbury Junior School, Southampton

A DAY IN THE LIFE OF A CAT

Oh great, fish again. I stretched my long, thin body and made my way to the living room. I sat next to my owner and watched TV.

After that I thought it was time to go for a walk. I went out of my cat flap and strolled around the block. I went around the park and then I came home and there was some milk and fish in my bowl. I finished my milk and fish and started to play with my toys.

The hot, boiling sun was shining on my black fur. I decided to take a quiet little sunbathing nap, dangling my tail over the wall, attracting many other cats.

Abigail Pearson (11)
Holbury Junior School, Southampton

A DAY IN THE LIFE OF AN OCTOPUS

I woke up with a mighty yawn and stretched my many legs, then I went to hunt down breakfast. I grabbed it and held it still with my powerful suckers.

After I had eaten my breakfast, I went to explore. A rusty metal cylinder hit me on the head. As I propelled myself through the waves, cuttlefish swam round me. I got so muddled trying to look at them, my eight legs got knotted. I hate it when that happens.

An hour later I finally got them untangled. The sun was setting, so I went to look for a nice rock to sleep on. Oh no, a fishing net, got to swim. Phew, I made it and there's a rock! *Yawn,* it's great living in the sea.

Thomas Last (10)
Holbury Junior School, Southampton

A DAY IN THE LIFE OF . . .

I woke up in the middle of the night sky. Peering into the trees and vines, I could hear waves crashing violently. I pulled the bare trees back and discovered the ocean. I waddled across the sea front and floated quietly, hiding from my enemies.

Suddenly, I could feel something or someone's jagged jaws gripping onto the lower part of my leg. I guessed it was a grey object, which was full of evil and extremely vicious teeth, I panicked and wondered what was I doing in the deeper end of the ocean? I tried to escape, but I was trapped. I was dragged under the water level, it was as dark as a dungeon and as evil as fire, but somehow was full of happiness, somewhere unexpected.

I never knew where I was but I always carried on, as if I was back home, eating my normal snacks, sleeping until five in the afternoon and celebrating my birthday, by stuffing lots of cakes, with my friends. I didn't want to know where I was, because it seemed so peaceful and calm, so I didn't see any problem with that. The best of it was that I would sizzle in the sun, lying on the golden sand, relaxing, as I sipped a refreshing cocktail which was topped with a red cherry as sweet as sugar and as sharp as glass.

Every day I would go picking flowers in the field, mostly poppies, then I would sell them.

Abbie Mitchener (11)
Holbury Junior School, Southampton

A DAY IN THE LIFE OF A DOG IN THE POUND

I woke up to hear a familiar voice, 'Breakfast time,' it said. It was my favourite food, pigs' ears and meat in jelly. I was only ever given it on special occasions, but what was the occasion? It wasn't my birthday and it definitely wasn't Christmas, because it was the middle of the summer, so why didn't I have the horrible cheap stuff, like normal?

Then it occurred to me. Maybe somebody was going to come and buy me. Wow! I stood up on my hind legs and shook my head around wildly, to get rid of any dust in my ears. I gulped down my breakfast and willingly went for a bath.

I heard that the people were coming to look at me at 12 o'clock. I had better be on my best behaviour, or else they might not want me. I wonder what it is like to have a loving owner?

I have just found out that they are on their way to my cage. I was getting really excited. Would they choose me? They came to my cage, big humans with big smiles. They handed some papers with pictures to my trainer and put a piece of material with a shiny, metal bone on it, around my neck and dragged me to a big lump of metal, called a car. A home at last!

Lois Wheeler (10)
Holbury Junior School, Southampton

A Day In A Life Of A Sock

'Hey! *Ouch!*' As me and my woolly partner were snatched by the most biggest spider I'd ever seen, whilst we were taken from our colourful drawer mates, as it pushed us into its lair, with wriggling toes arguing with each second and sweaty foot odour wafting through my nose! It couldn't get any worse!

Phwoor! What a stink! I remember when I was a nice, clean, new sock. No smells and no manky toenails! A sock can only wish. Save me, save me!

Argh! That was the last thing we said before we were gulped by a giant spinning monster, crushing young socklings with its powerful teeth.

Emily Heron (11)
Holbury Junior School, Southampton

A DAY IN THE LIFE OF A SOCK

Ow! Someone has opened me up again . . . *argh!* There's a big giant squishing me.

Oh no! What's that smell? *Urgh* stinky! Get me out of here!

Ouch! Ow! What on earth are the stupid lumps doing? *Ow!* Stop fighting will you? You're hurting me! Those little lumps are causing trouble again!

Elisha Dixon (11)
Holbury Junior School, Southampton

A DAY IN THE LIFE OF A CARPET!

'Owww!' It's the four-legged creatures, they're back. What gives them the right to scratch me with their sharp claws and leave squeaky toys, covered in smelly slobber, all over me?

Oh no! Here comes the usual 4pm muck parade. Large, flat, rubber things stomp all over me, leaving trails of brown stuff everywhere. If that isn't enough, the monster makes the creatures roll around, rubbing their dirty fur into me . . . the smell is awful.

'Ow, ow ow!' They've gone, but here comes the deadly sucker on wheels. *Vroom, vroom!* It's sucking me up. *Ouch!* My hair! It rips the mud from my cosy fluff and the rotten earwax from my ears. It feels like I've done ten rounds with Mike Tyson.

It's got late. The new living thing was making a screeching noise. I opened my tired eyes and caught a quick glimpse of baby Barry's bottom before . . . what's that repulsive smell? I was soaked to the bone! To make matters worse, somebody rubbed my face with a spiky thing that scratched me sore. The pain still didn't remove the terrible smell. It smelt like a skunk!

I finally got some sleep, but the next day was no better!

Skye Wright (11)
Holbury Junior School, Southampton

A DAY IN THE LIFE OF A HAMSTER

Silent as usual, then suddenly, big giants invade my world. (So I wake up for my daily entertainment).

Later I go to get breakfast (nuts again). Then I suddenly had a quenching thirst for water. My water tank was empty. *Annoyed!* In frustration (and a little pain) I went down to the bottom floor for a tiddle, when the monster came back with more water.

Then a huge, spider-like hand came towards me. *Ow!* He's squeezing too hard. In agony, I bit one of his hairy (dirty as well) fingers. Suddenly, he let go and I was falling! I landed on my wheel. Next time I won't just bite his finger!

Michael Switzer (10)
Holbury Junior School, Southampton

A Day In A Life Of A Refrigerator

Ow! Something's squashing me.

Eww! Ice cream is dribbling down my back again . . . I'm annoyed with them. Human beings keep on opening me up and making me ill, by shoving sickly food in my tummy. I would not dare to stand in sunlight today, I would die. Why is heat so popular?

Ouch! Chicken legs are trampling over me again. They have got a lot of fat on them, haven't they . . . they need to diet!

Phew! It's getting really hot in here, I'm burning up.

Suddenly, five tiny, wiggle worms approached me and switched me off! I felt sick. My tummy hurt. Everything around me was blurred. I couldn't speak . . . my breathing hurt . . . I think this is it . . .

Suzanne Sayce (11)
Holbury Junior School, Southampton

THE DAY OF A LIFE OF A SOFA

As I luckily see light, a tall clump falls on me.

They think I don't have feelings, but I do and then he puts on a glowing type of thing.

Suddenly, I feel a rumble. *Err!* It stinks! I hope someone gets me away from this stench.

Splash! I hope that wasn't what I think it was . . . *Err!* It was. Milk and cereal, not my favourite!

Finally, I was free. *Whoa!* I was levitating outside. *Bang!* I was outside. *Whoa!* I was moving again. Cool! I was with my old friend, chair, but he had a broken leg, I knew this was bad news for me.

I saw a clump charging towards me, with a shiny piece of metal, *argh!*

Grant Morgan (11)
Holbury Junior School, Southampton

THE DAY AND THE LIFE OF A SKATEBOARD

As I struggle with this fiend on my back, I also try to slow down my feet. *Gross!* I have got some sticky, pink stuff on my foot again. *Nuts!* My foot has fallen off again, if only he would listen, but he ignores me and pushes on my rear end and I see light but my bum is sore.

After half an hour, the fiend jumps off me, like a jack-in-the-box and then I was rolling, like a hot wheel.

What is this? It is a kind of creature. *Hey!* Wait! The fiend is leaving me. Well, that's a relief, so I guess I am on my own. Well, I think the place is clear.

Hey! The rolling creature is coming back. I think he is going . . . *argh!*

James McLaughlin (11)
Holbury Junior School, Southampton

A Day In A Life Of A Carrier Bag

'Would you like any help packing, Madam?' I heard the lady on the till say to the smelly customer. A big hand digs in and grabs me by the tummy. *Urgh!* Sprouts! They're making me eat sprouts and cabbage. The customer picks me up by my white, cold ears, with their sweaty hands and dumps me in a dark and spooky place.

The ride was very bumpy and I thought I was going to be sick. Then we enter a warm, cosy room and they dig their hands down my throat and pull out the sprouts and cabbage. *Uh-oh!* I'm heading for the bin.

Look! I'm at the recycling factory once again. I'm heading for the Tesco's stamping machine. I'm at the bottom of the bag tub. Finally, I can go to sleep.

Nicola Duhig (11)
Holbury Junior School, Southampton

A DAY IN THE LIFE OF A CARPET

Oh no! Here they come again . . . *Ow! Ooh!* Hey! How dare you trample on me and mess up my lovely red fluff.

When I had just woken up, a 'miniature' giant came crawling all over me and what was worse, as it was staring down at me, a big waterfall of goo came pouring down . . . s*plat!*

Next thing I knew (even though it is good to take your shoes off) this 'fat' giant kicked hers off and wiggled her fat, porkie things and . . . *phwoar!* What a pong!

Oh, how I wish I was back in those days when me and my mates lived in a massive house, full of different sizes, colours and quality. Well, it was better than here anyway!

Yeah, life as a carpet is only cool when you are actually cleaned and looked after, for Hoover's sake!

Carmen Lever (10)
Holbury Junior School, Southampton

A Day In The Life Of A Sock

Ow! Someone threw me in a tunnel. *Yuck!* I am getting all soggy. I am all sweaty and sick of getting dirty. I am absolutely fed up with getting ripped and getting even more tacky every day. I hate getting hung every time after being in the tunnel.

Every single day there is two certain lumps that argue. They never stop arguing. I also hate being shut away after they have hung me.

Ow! Someone just threw me in the tunnel again. Once again, soggy and wet. If I could run away, I would. Now look, shut away in a drawer.

Ow! Another one of me has just wrapped round my neck. I am getting sick of this. Out again and now the lumps are going in me. Now I am going in a dark hole and now I am lifting up into the air.

Jade Perks (10)
Holbury Junior School, Southampton

A Day In The Life Of A Sewer!

Ow! Someone flushed their chain again. I hate it when that happens! My body is revolting. It stinks like toxic waste and rats are running all over me . . .

It's worse when I get blocked up. Long things shoving pipes down me. Rude rats leave their mess all over me and long, brown things shoot past me.

Clumps of wet, squishy stuff piles up and won't move, annoying!

One of my worst things, is when little, scaly creatures with eyes, float past me and they smell nasty!

Daniel Lee & Brendan Jones (11)
Holbury Junior School, Southampton

A DAY IN THE LIFE OF ARTHUR REID

Hi! I'm Arthur. I live with my mum, my dad and my sister, DW. Normally I start the day like this: my dad makes pancakes for breakfast, after that, I go to the arcades with Buster. At 10 o'clock, we both cycle to school.

We have a long assembly, then we start class. Our teacher, Mr Ratburn, gives us a maths hour and half of our literacy hour. At 11 o'clock we get recess, and lunch for 30 minutes. At 2 o'clock, we do history. In history, we're studying the Anglo-Saxons. I think they're great.

At 3.30 we have soccer trials. At school, I'm in the soccer team, it's great fun.
Today it's really unlucky because my best friend's got a detention.

After school, my team have a soccer match. Yeah! School's over, now for the footie . . . as usual, we lose 4-3, but I got three though. I told Dad and he's really glad.

'Mum,' I called, 'DW's being annoying.'
'DW, come down here,' Mum said.
By the way, I'm in the middle of homework.

I got to bed at 8.30, it has just gone half-eight. Goodnight.

Thomas Gillespie (9)
St Mary Star of the Sea Catholic Primary School, St Leonards-on-sea

ONE DAY IN THE LIFE OF . . .

A little pony, smaller than you, was walking in her stable and she caught sight of a young unicorn. It was a beautiful yellow colour unicorn with purple hair flowing back behind her and a multicoloured spike.

Hannah, the pony, went off and galloped to this unicorn whose name was Jasmine and neighed, 'Do you want to come back with me?'
'Yes please, I would love to.'
So they both galloped back to the stable.

The pony stopped the unicorn and they landed in a world full of sweets. The pony asked the unicorn where they were. He answered politely, 'We are in the world of animal sweets.
'Are they really all sweets?'
'Yes they are. Do you want to live here?'
'I would love to.'
'Well, we'd better start building our house,' said the unicorn politely.

So off they went to get some sweetie sticks to build their house. Soon they had enough long sticks and they started building a lovely little cottage. When it was done, they started looking for some sweetie straw. With that, they could make the roof. The roof was soon made. They stood and stared at it and suddenly it caught fire. They ran for their lives, up a ladder that took them to the stable.
'That happened because I'm a magic unicorn. Any unicorn with a multicoloured spike is magic.'

Rachel Bone (8)
St Mary Star of the Sea Catholic Primary School, St Leonards-on-sea

THE DAY EDWARD DIED

One day, Edward woke up feeling unreal and giddy. His wife was calling him downstairs.

'Come on, Edward,' she screamed.

Edward quietly whispered, 'Coming deary,' in terror.

When Edward had finished his pottage, he set off to the butcher's to do his job. When Edward arrived at the butcher's the other people who worked there were dead and hung on the hooks where the meat was meant to hang. There was blood dripping on the floor making spills. Then Edward screamed in shock, horror and terror at the same time. Edward saw people running out of the back door, so legged after them. He took two of the butcher's knives. Edward didn't know that the murderers were mysterious, spooky ghosts. Edward never found the two ghosts, so he went home to find his wife with blood dripping from her head.

Edward remembered that he had two people put to death because they were causing havoc at the butcher's. They were called Thomas and Henry Watson. Edward was scared, he thought they might be haunting him, making his life miserable, then they would kill him.

Edward would not step out of the house. When Edward was sleeping, he heard a noise. It was Thomas and Henry with a sharp axe. They chopped Edward's head off and there was blood all over the bed. Edwards was now dead. Now Edward haunts the Watson family for revenge.

Mark Longmire (9)
St Mary Star of the Sea Catholic Primary School, St Leonards-on-sea

THE HAUNTED HOUSE

One night I saw a house which had been haunted for twenty-five years, and my friend and I dared each other to go in there. We started to go in, when we heard a thump and a scream and I went to see where the scream came from. My friend said he would be just behind me, but he was scared, so he left me and ran back home. I was all alone in the spooky house and I heard a scream from the attic. Then I went slowly to the attic door. My hair was sticking up on end. I opened the door, there were goosebumps on my arms.

I saw some tiny stairs leading up to the roof. I quickly walked up the stairs, my body was shaking from my toes up to my hair. I saw a hole in the roof and I saw in front of me, an old lady screaming. She was the owner of the house and she had been captured by the ghost. She was tied up in chains. Beside her was a soldier ghost, he was in his uniform. He turned around and I pushed him off the roof. He fell down to the ground and died a second time. As I was looking at his body, it disappeared into the ground.

As this was happening, a bunch of keys floated up to me. I caught them and unlocked the old lady. She was so happy, she gave me a cookie and I ran all the way home.

As I ran through my back door, I shouted, '*Mum*, you won't believe what I did tonight . . .'

William Calcott-James (8)
St Mary Star of the Sea Catholic Primary School, St Leonards-on-sea

THE TARTAN TATTOOED TIGER

Long ago in Asia, there lived a king who had a tiger with a tattoo on its back. They were not just friends, but were partners. Wherever the king went, the tiger went.

One evening, a messenger arrived saying that Indians were travelling down for war. The king called for the first troops in Asia. Every carpenter in Asia was to come and make swords, shields, bows and arrows.

The Indians arrived twelve months later. By then, all the Asian troops were ready. The long, tiring battle was vicious and gruesome, until there were only two left of the Asian troops: the king and the tiger. They were both hanged on a mountain staring over the extremely beautiful palace. The Indians skinned the tiger with the tattoo of three black scars remaining on the skin.

That night there was a big thunderstorm and the mists formed the tiger's ghost. It was coming towards the Indians' night camp. It burst into flames. The tiger grinned at the sight of the troops burning. The rest who survived, fled in fear of the tiger's tremendous growl!

Elliot Simmons (9)
St Mary Star of the Sea Catholic Primary School, St Leonards-on-sea

A TERRIBLE DEATH

I lay in my comfortable bed alone, then I heard a creepy sound. I looked around the dark room, I saw something white. Hope it didn't see me. Then I heard somebody say, 'Kill! I will kill you, murder!' So I just went back to bed.

Next day, I was walking (well, running) and in the next second, I was in a sack! It was totally black and I was really scared. Then I found I was locked in a high-up room.

A slinky, tall man came in the room. He had an axe in one hand and a sharp knife in the other. He pointed the sharp knife at my throat and with the axe, he cut my head off. I was dead! The whole of my family was extremely sad.

I now roam round frightening people myself.

Charlotte Dowling (9)
St Mary Star of the Sea Catholic Primary School, St Leonards-on-sea

CASPER THE FRIENDLY GHOST TRIES TO FIND A FRIEND

One day Casper, the friendly ghost, went out to find a friend to play with, but he didn't find anyone until he came across a big house. The house was very big and spooky-looking. He was sure he would find some ghost friends in there.

He went through the door of the big, scary-looking house. He couldn't find any ghosts, but in one room, fast asleep, was a little human girl. She had black hair and brown eyes. She looked very friendly to Casper. He went closer to the bed. Suddenly the little girl woke up and sat up in her bed. She said, 'Dad, are you there?'
Casper said, 'No, it's me. Casper,' and she screamed.
Her dad came in and said, 'What is it?'
'There's a ghost in my room.'
'Where?'
'Over there.'
'There is no ghost in this house, go back to sleep. It's 2 o'clock in the morning.'

When the little girl woke up, Casper was floating above her. She was about to scream again, but Casper got a scarf to wrap around her mouth. 'Please don't be scared,' he said. 'I won't hurt you. I am looking for a friend. My name is Casper, what is yours?'
She was trying to say her name, but she couldn't because she had the scarf around her mouth. Casper took off the scarf and she told him her name, it was Jen.

From then on, Jen had her very own secret, special friend. Casper, the friendly ghost.

Ashleigh Humberstone (9)
St Mary Star of the Sea Catholic Primary School, St Leonards-on-sea

THE HAUNTED SCHOOL KIDNAP

The school bell went very loudly and the girls and boys started to come in the classroom. The teacher came in. They got down to work and some mysterious tapping went on.
Sam said, 'Who is that tapping?'

Just before they all went to the hall for lunch, the mysterious ghost kidnapped a boy called Sam because he didn't like him. Sam screamed and shouted, *'Help!'* but no one heard.
The freaky ghost called out, 'I want to kill you.'

Meanwhile in the classroom, the teacher started to worry about Sam. She asked people in the classroom where he had got to. Suddenly, the teacher went looking and could not find him and so she ran into the staffroom and screamed, 'One of our boys is missing,' and everyone started to look.

They found him lying on the floor in the shed and calling, *'Help.'* But then he didn't talk again and his pulse went. They wanted to find out what happened and the ghost wanted someone else.

Rhian Jones (9)
St Mary Star of the Sea Catholic Primary School, St Leonards-on-sea

THE GHOST WHO TAPPED TWO TIMES

One day I was sitting in the classroom. We were in the middle of maths and someone tapped. I turned around and Jessica, my worst enemy was behind me. I said, 'Hey, don't do that!'
'What?' Jessica shouted.
'Tap me on the back!'
'I didn't!'
'Yes you did, you liar.'
'Girls, stop that now!' the teacher commanded.
We stopped then.

The next day, I sat next to Franchesca. She is my best friend. This time we were in the middle of English and I felt someone tap me. I knew it wasn't Franchesca, because she wouldn't do that. I knew it was something, so at break, I decided to got to the attic and have a look at what was there.

First, I had to sneak a ladder from Mr Scott's room. I thought there was a ladder in there. Luckily, Year 6 were out singing, so I could go in the entrance to the attic from their room.

In there, I heard a ghost, so I ran down the ladder and called the ghost hunters straight away. They came in about an hour after I called them. I showed them the way up. They had a funny-looking machine, but I did not care. I just wanted them to get the ghost.

It took about three hours to catch the ghost. After they went, I never felt a tap again.

Osian Veall (8)
St Mary Star of the Sea Catholic Primary School, St Leonards-on-sea

Fairy Tale

Long, long ago in medieval England, a princess lived. Her name was Edith. She was considered the most beautiful in the land. A lot of knights and princes wanted to marry her. None of them truly loved her, they just wanted to marry her for all the riches she had and so that they could be king. There was only one knight who truly loved her, his name was Arthur. They never got to see each other as Arthur was always away fighting.

The night before Arthur was due to fight in the woods behind Edith's house, Arthur asked for her hand in marriage. Edith did not know what to say, so she told him she would think about it.

The next day, Arthur wasn't fighting his best because he was thinking about Edith.

Edith had just woken up and heard the fighting. She ran out into the woods behind her castle. She called out, 'Arthur!' but it was too late, a sword had just been plunged into his stomach. The second he fell to the ground, Edith died of heartbreak.

She still roams around the woods to this very day, calling, 'Yes! Yes!' to Arthur's grave.

Sarah Wainwright (9)
St Mary Star of the Sea Catholic Primary School, St Leonards-on-sea

MY POWER

Hi, my name's Mark. Since I was born, I've had this birthmark. It's kind of like a black lightning scar, with three lines coming out of it. I'll tell you what it means. In Greek mythology, it says it's the sign of Hercules. I'm super strong and it gets bad. I've got a girlfriend called Lisa and if she saw this, she'd know I have super strength. She's an expert about this stuff! I don't want her to know.

One day, this carnival arrived unexpectedly. Lisa and me got to it at six o'clock in the evening and guess what? It was closed!

Two weeks later, two kids were kidnapped and a piece of paper was left next to where they had been kidnapped, signed 'Dr Evil'. I had to do something, after all, I am super strong. I had to go to the carnival and find out for myself!

One night at 12.30 (12.29 to be precise), I went to the carnival. I thought there would be some climbing involved, but it turned out that the gates were open. I walked in and went on for a bit, and then I heard a noise behind me, *Dr Evil!* What he was staring at was a skeleton, and on Dr Evil's right arm there was a tattoo the same as my birthmark!
'Ha ha, you care to challenge me?'
'Bring it on!'
He lunged at me and pulled out a knife. I should not have said that!

Elinor Adie (8)
St Mary Star of the Sea Catholic Primary School, St Leonards-on-sea

GHOST STORY

Two more days till we buy our house. We have just had a phone call and they said, 'You can come to buy your house now.'

As soon as we stepped in, there was a massive, deep, dark, black hole and we fell down it. I fell through this pale white thing. Luckily I landed safely and I looked up and saw this terribly scary ghost. It came down about three hundred miles an hour. It out-stared me!

Dad then fell on me and I broke my arm. The ghost went up through the hole and got a first-aid kit and brought it down to Dad. Dad opened the box and it had a bomb in. Dad picked up the bomb to chuck it at the ghost but he blew himself up! The ghost picked Dad up and the ghost then chucked Dad up in the air and gobbled him down. You could see dad going down the ghost's throat! Then the ghost was gobbling Dad.

I found a BB gun. I was shooting it at the ghost. I found this bright orange book which said on it, *'The Spell Book,'* so I ran up to it and I recited a spell and the ghost went away into the book. Dad came out all in one piece!

In the end, we didn't buy the house!

Louis Friedlander (9)
St Mary Star of the Sea Catholic Primary School, St Leonards-on-sea

THE HAUNTED SCHOOL

In a school in the south east of England, a ghost hid in the shed. He had died on Hallowe'en, he was killed by his best friend. This is how it happened.

His name was Perry. Perry's friend Daniel called him over and then stuffed him in the shed. In the morning, he went to Year 4, picked up a board pen and wrote, 'Better watch your backs.'
With a raging roar of a scream, the head came in and said, 'I need to talk to you all, I have found a body, it belongs to Perry. Somebody has been really evil.'
No one in Year 4 believed her.

At lunchtime, a boy was killed. Everyone saw what happened, he was turned into a part of a monster. Everyone was frightened. Then a girl was found dead in the bathroom. She became the second half of the monster. The monster was a vampire that could shoot bats. Suddenly, the children could see Perry as a ghost floating around. Everyone was sent home.

In the cold rustling of the night, the vampire was turned into two ghosts.

The next day, most of the students came to school. The ghosts entered the boring classroom of Year 4 and wrote on the board, 'Where is he?' The person they were looking for was Daniel Simons. He was on holiday. Everyone was sent home for a month because of the school being haunted.

When they went back to school, the children could feel that the horrible ghosts were gone.

Robert Clifford (9)
St Mary Star of the Sea Catholic Primary School, St Leonards-on-sea

THE SCHOOL GHOST

'I'm the school ghost and I'm going to make war between you and your friends.'

'Jennie, stop tapping me on the shoulder.'
'I'm not, stop accusing me of tapping you when I'm not.'
'I'm not your friend.'
'I'm not yours either.'

'I've just made all of the school not friends,' sniggered the ghost.

'Mrs Stroud, isn't it strange that none of the people in the class are friends anymore? Shall we call the detectors to come to the school?'

The detectors came and scanned the school and they found a ghost. When they looked on the scale, he was off the chart. If they hadn't captured him in time, he was going to *kill* me, Diva-Lee Braine. The detectives said that the ghost was so evil, he could take over the whole world. He had enough power to cause everyone in the world to fight and to be an unfriendly world. He would have caused the greatest war of all time. We were so lucky that no one got hurt.

I was so scared, but at least I went home for five days while they checked the whole school. After the five days, the school re-opened and everyone came back in a good mood.

Now, everyone can make friends again.

Diva-Lee Braine (9)
St Mary Star of the Sea Catholic Primary School, St Leonards-on-sea

MY DIARY

Hello, my name's Lilly and I come from France and well, I was in my room doing my homework (like always) and something or someone was in my room and I did not know what to do. OK, I did know what to do, so just scream! (And shout!) *'There's something in my room!'*
Suddenly, something said to me, 'My name's Gregory.'
'Argh! There's a ghost in my room!'

My mummy hurried up the stairs and said, 'What was all that screaming for?'
'Well Mummy, I saw a g-g-ghost in my room.'
'There's no such thing as ghosts, and you're grounded for making such a terrible noise.'
So I went to my desk and cried very loudly. She didn't believe me. I said to myself, 'I'm not scared of the ghost anymore.'
Suddenly a voice said, 'Would you like to be my friend?'
I shivered and replied, 'OK,' in a scared voice.

'How did you know that?' the ghost said.
'Because you said it a minute ago,' I muttered.
'Oh, I didn't know that,' he said.
'So are you a ghost?' I asked.
'Yes.'
'Oh my goodness,' I replied.
Then the ghost said, 'Don't start screaming again, or your mum will be up here. So what's your name?'
'Lilly.'
'Lilly, do you have a computer game called 'Ghost'? That's where I live. I got sucked out of my world through a time machine and I need to get back.'

They went to Lilly's computer and it said, '10, 9, 8, 7, 6, 5, 4, 3, 2, 1.'
The ghost turned to Lilly and said, 'This is the time to say goodbye.' He twisted and twirled into the computer and was gone.

Melodie Bright (9)
St Mary Star of the Sea Catholic Primary School, St Leonards-on-sea

GHOST STORY

One night I was in bed reading an old, scary-looking book. I was trying to get to sleep. Suddenly, a see-through ghost appeared. It said, 'Save yourself from the headless horseman. He wants to kill you for a head.'

The next day I woke up with a headache anyway. I rushed to get everything on, then I rushed outside to fight the headless horseman. The headless horseman came behind me with a sharp axe. I shot like a bullet and dived under him. He charged at me again. I ducked under the axe and kicked him in the body. By then, he was getting really mad. I had to rush into the house and lock the door. Then I had to run upstairs and lock my bedroom door. I heard a noise downstairs, it was the headless horseman banging against the locked, white door.

'Come downstairs, Sam,' Mum shouted.

'Oh no,' I said, worrying about Mum and Dad.

I ran downstairs and told Mum and Dad, but they didn't believe me. But when the headless horseman slammed his axe through the door, we shot upstairs like bullets. We all ran in different rooms. I was in my room.

Suddenly the ghost appeared again and gave me a hoover. I ran out of my room and sucked him up. I locked the hoover in a cupboard and he was never seen again.

Sam McShane (9)
St Mary Star of the Sea Catholic Primary School, St Leonards-on-sea

THE DRAGON AND THE ARMY

Once upon a time, there was a king and queen. The story starts when the king and the queen were eating dinner. Suddenly, ghosts popped in and out of the walls and just as suddenly, the candles went out. The king and the queen were terrified. They ran onto the balcony, when they saw a whole army coming to invade. They sent out their army. They fought a ferocious battle, but they won.

The dragon heard about them losing. He was furious, so he flew over. It took many days until finally he got to the castle. When he was there, he rested until morning. In the morning, he remembered what had happened, so he broke into the castle and snatched the princess from her bedroom and took her back to his lair.

The king was sad when he found out, so he sent out his men to go and retrieve the princess. They came back in fifty days. They had killed the dragon and rescued the princess. The king and the queen were so happy, they just needed a bit more help from their knights. They had rescued the princess, so the king had to let them free, but there was one more thing. Guess what it was that they had to do? Scare the ghosts from the kitchen.

Daniel Gillespie (8)
St Mary Star of the Sea Catholic Primary School, St Leonards-on-sea

A FRIENDLY LITTLE GHOST

One night I heard a rattling noise. It was Friday the thirteenth. I was going to be unlucky. Then suddenly, a kind-looking ghost popped up at my feet (just the head).
She said, 'Hello, I'm Mildred.'
Soon after that, we made friends.

Me and Mildred went out of my window. She explained why. She wanted to capture the evil ghost of Hastings. As soon as we saw him, he was busy at work, haunting a sweet little girl. Mildred had a bag of ghost-shrinking powder. Mildred didn't touch it because she was a ghost.
'That horrible, ugly ghost hasn't seen us yet,' I whispered to Mildred.
The ghost came down low.
'Oh no! He's seen us.'

Me and Mildred ran and ran as fast as we could. When we stopped, he stopped, so we threw the powder at him and it went in his mouth. Then as quick as a flash, he shrank and was the size of a rubber, so we put him in a pot and I still have him in that pot.

Mildred still visits me. She's not the only ghost I've seen, but she is the friendliest one!

Jennifer Meredith (9)
St Mary Star of the Sea Catholic Primary School, St Leonards-on-sea

THE HAUNTED HOUSE

This is the story of a man ghost who died in a big old house. He comes back to life as a ghost and freaks out a little girl and her uncle.

On the 13th of August, history repeats itself from 100 years ago. At midnight, darkness falls and a great big *boom*. The basement door opens slowly with a creak, but there is no sign of anyone coming out. Then suddenly, the girl called Ellie, wakes up and sees her door opening and in comes black blur. It goes through Ellie and she fearfully looks behind her. There is nothing there, so in flash, she dives under her bed covers.

Soon it is morning and her uncle finds her balanced on top of a radio mysteriously on her knees, asleep. She walks up with her eyes glowing red. With her eyes, she stares at her uncle. He starts to shake as she walks out of her bedroom door to eat her breakfast. She stares at her uncle and she starts to shake her eyes as she is evilly daydreaming. Her eyes keep on flashing yellow. After she has finished her breakfast, she walks back up to her bedroom and looks in the mirror. Then she realises that she is going weird in the head.

She makes herself scared by thinking of what she saw that night. Her uncle thinks it's an evil spirit in the house, because it is very old and people could have died in this house.

When her uncle comes to her bedroom at night, she is screaming and floating in the air, staring at a spot in the room. Ellie's uncle looks at the spot and realises what she is scared of. It is a black man staring eye to eye with her, laughing in a dead evil way. In a flash, Ellie falls to the ground and the man ghost disappears.

The uncle decides the only way to save Ellie is to move house. Ellie and her uncle find a brand new house which no one has lived in.

But what will happen to the next people in the house?

Bethany Groombridge (9)
St Mary Star of the Sea Catholic Primary School, St Leonards-on-sea

THE HEADLESS HORSEMAN

One night in a house, it was the 31st of October. At 8pm, a man named Thomas was preparing for trick or treaters. He suddenly heard a strange noise. Thomas went to find out what the noise was. The sound got louder and louder. He stopped there, he could hear it but not see it. He went over to the wall. He heard an, *'Nanaaa.'* It was outside, so Thomas went outside to find out what it was.

When Thomas had got outside, behind his house he saw a black horse with a man on it. Thomas was out of his mind. The man turned around, Thomas was scared even more now, because he had no head.
The man said, 'Give me your head. I am the headless horseman.'
Thomas was even more terrified. Thomas sprinted and sprinted till he got away from the headless, ugly thing.

After that, the headless horsemen took an axe out of his neck and then ran after Thomas. 'Naaa, naaa,' the headless horseman charged after Thomas. Thomas had to think of a way to get rid of him. He thought and could think of three ways. 1, run away till it was light and hope he went away. 2, phone the police, but he could be killed before he got to the phone or while he was on the phone, or 3, he could kill him himself.

Thomas went with number 3, and he ran behind a tree. The headless horseman walked along past him on his horse and with an axe in his left hand, Thomas ran out, killed the headless man and his horse and buried them.

Thomas ran inside panicking. Seeing a light, he saw the headless horseman and he went into the moon.
'Ha, ha, next year Thomas. Next year I'll kill you.'

Ryan Byas (9)
St Mary Star of the Sea Catholic Primary School, St Leonards-on-sea

GHOST STORY

One day I was doing my homework. Suddenly, a ghost popped out from somewhere. He told me to go with him, so I did. He took me to a spooky, creepy castle which was haunted.
I asked, 'Why are we here?'
He said, 'This is my home. I would like you to meet my family. Come inside.'

There was his mum, dad, two brothers, two sisters and uncle and auntie. I got freaked out. I felt as if I was going to faint. They were going to become evil, so I ran as fast as a cheetah. They came chasing after me. I found a little hole in a very old, locked-up cupboard, so I climbed in the cupboard through the hole. The ghost family ran past the old cupboard. I got out. I screamed. I had cobwebs all over me, with disgusting creepy spiders. They heard me scream. I ran out of the spooky, creepy castle.

I went back home. My mum nearly had a fit when she saw the state of me. All the creepy spiders fell off me and onto my mum's best new carpet. They all crept into the dining room where all our pets and my seven and two-year-old brothers were feeding the lizard, chameleon and fish. I screamed because the spiders from the creepy castle went in the lizard and chameleon and fish's cricket box and fish food.

I grabbed my seven-year-old brother and told him about the ghost. He said I'd got to tell Mum, so I told her. It wasn't a pretty sight. We had to rush Mum to the hospital because she'd fainted and she wouldn't wake up. I asked Dad if I was in big trouble.
He said, 'No, you are in *huge* trouble.'
I was grounded for a month.

Jessica Martin (9)
St Mary Star of the Sea Catholic Primary School, St Leonards-on-sea

THE VAMPIRE FAMILY

One day, Jake and Ann came back home from being at school all day and being out with their friends afterwards. They came home into their room, then they turned the telly on. But behind the television, they saw a very dark black shadow. The shadow started talking, it was saying, 'Come with me Ann, come with me Jake.'

Ann and Jake were huddled up together on the sofa. They were terrified. Ann and Jake didn't know what the talking black shadow was. They were so afraid, they went with the shadow. The shadow led them up a bumpy, twisting path, it seemed to go on forever and ever. The path started going up a hill and a few minutes later, they were above the clouds. At last they came to something which was a funny shape. When it came a bit clearer, they saw it was a castle. The black shadow led Ann and Jake up to the door and let them in. Then the shadow flew off and left Ann and Jake on their own.

They crept inside the door and found a coffin. Very slowly, they opened the coffin and out popped four vampires and two animals. Ann and Jake were very scared, but then they realised that it was their mum, dad, baby sister, baby brother, cat and dog.
'Mum, Dad, Charlie (baby brother), Zoe (baby sister), dog and cat!' said Ann and Jake.
'Hello Ann and Jake,' Mum replied, joyfully.
Then they all heard a creak upstairs.

They went up and opened the cupboard. Out came glowing eyes and red hands. It was . . .

Kimberley Pain (8)
St Mary Star of the Sea Catholic Primary School, St Leonards-on-sea

TIME TRAVEL TOUR

One day, Ann got up and she went downstairs to eat breakfast. Her brother James was down there. Her mum said, 'We are going to the park today.' So Ann and James went upstairs to get changed.

When they got to the park, they saw something behind the tree. Ann and James got caught in it. James found out soon enough that it was a time machine. First they went into the past. They fell from the sky onto a street, Ann nearly broke her arm. Ann and James met a man on the street, he had stolen a necklace from a jewellery store. James had noticed that he wore very strange clothes and the children played with funny toys. Next, James and Ann went into a sweet shop. They were giving free samples. James said, 'Cool, I am going to try one,' but spat it right out. Then suddenly he said, 'These sweets are disgusting.'
'Oh well,' said Ann. 'Come on, we have to find a way out of here.'
'OK,' said James.

Then suddenly they went back into the time travel machine and this time, they went into the future. This time they fell on to a flying truck with cushions on it. There were lots of flying cars there. But when the fun was just starting, they woke up and it was all a dream.

Sofia Whitaker (8)
St Mary Star of the Sea Catholic Primary School, St Leonards-on-sea

A Day In The Life Of A Ghost

Everyone is scared of Frankenstein because Frankenstein once appeared in 1975, cowboy time. His parents died. A man and a girl saw him and made him evil, after that, no one saw him again. In 2003, they say he lives in the haunted house down at the crossroads.

Two boys, Mat and Joe, lived down the road too. They were not scared, Frankenstein was a legend some people didn't believe, so they went to the haunted house. Before they opened the door, a bat came flying out, but they thought it was a big, long, toy on a string bat.

They walked in, Jo got scared as they walked in and they saw a man. He was scary, they thought he was a statue, but he wasn't, he was real and Jo got goosebumps. The man who was sitting on the chair was Frankenstein. He got up. Jo and Mat did not see him, so that meant they were in big trouble. Frankenstein woke up from Hell. He grabbed a knife and tried to kill them. Wait a minute . . . bad ending.

'Would you like a cup of tea?' said Frankenstein.
Jo and Mat turned around and said, 'Are you Frankenstein?'
'Yes I am,' he said.
'Are you evil?'
'No. Well, I was, but now I'm good. Are you OK?'
'No, I feel sick,' said Mat.
'Go on and leave me.'
'Sorry, I'll leave, and see you in Heaven.'

William Oshuntoki (7)
St Mary Star of the Sea Catholic Primary School, St Leonards-on-sea

THE STORY OF TERROR TOWER

A few years ago, there lived a cleaner and an old lady. They lived in a castle in London. One night, the cleaner went to the top of the castle to clean a room which had not ever been cleaned before. When she got there, she felt a squeeze on her shoulder. When the cleaner turned to see what it was, she found there was nobody there. So down the stairs she went, as fast as she could. Now that was all true. The cleaner told the lady about it. She didn't ever go up to the attic where the room was again.

The next night, they were awoken by the noise of a dog barking at midnight, so the lady and the cleaner went down to see what it was. When they got down, there was nothing there except a burning candle which blew out all by itself. After a few seconds, they heard a voice which said, 'Come and join us.' They sat down, but the ghosts ate them alive.

The next morning, the ghosts killed everyone except a butcher who lived right next door to the terror tower. You would have thought they would have got him first.

A few years after, the terror tower has been turned into an amusement park where lots of people go. Some people come out half alive. Scientists have found a note that says, 'Ghosts of the past beware!' Some people have fallen in the Forever Dungeon and died. Not one has ever come out alive. Do you believe me? Sound very spooky, hey?

Lauren Henson (8)
St Mary Star of the Sea Catholic Primary School, St Leonards-on-sea

THE WEIRD CASTLES

A dragon had come to the castle and he broke the castle and the princess and the prince had to get out of the castle, so they got another castle. But there was a ghost that really scared them, so they had to get another castle. But that castle had a very bad man, so the prince tried to fight him, but the prince got hurt. So the princess took up the prince's sword and killed the bad man and helped the prince. They lived happily ever after.

Andrew Russell (8)
St Mary Star of the Sea Catholic Primary School, St Leonards-on-sea

A DAY IN THE LIFE OF A PING-PONG BALL

Once, a boy was in his living room playing ping pong. He really enjoyed his ping-pong set. He whacked it out of the window. The boy peered out of the window and shouted, 'Oh no!' in such a sad voice. The ball bounced down the road, then *wham!* It hit a bump straight on, it hurtled through the air and bashed into a wall. It hit the floor and bounced down the road in a flash.

'Phew,' he muttered. 'Wow! I can talk . . .' Then he was plunged into total darkness.

Splash! He was underwater for a minute, then he bobbed back up. He bobbed along for what seemed like hours. Suddenly, he came to a halt. Hundreds upon hundreds of rats were scampering about. Surprisingly he saw an individual rat sitting alone. He went to the rat and said, 'Hello.'
'Hello,' muttered the rodent.
'What's your name?'
'Damien,' he replied.
'Why are you so sad?'
'I want to be a pet.'
'Right, pleased to meet you. Come with me, I'll help.'
'OK,' he said, and off they went.

They went on and saw a light. As they drew closer, they saw it was a hole. Damien scampered up the wall and went through the hole. The ball jumped up and they were all in broad daylight.

They carried on their journey and met a dog. They talked and the dog agreed to take them to his master. His master was eight. He agreed to look after them.

Jackson Mann (8)
St Mary Star of the Sea Catholic Primary School, St Leonards-on-sea

SCARY SUMMER CAMP

'I don't feel up to this, Calvin,' said Daisy when she was packing her bags.
'Don't say that,' said Calvin. 'Mum's going too.'
Daisy and Calvin are going to summer camp with their mum.

'Right then kids, it's time to go,' shouted Daisy and Calvin's mum. So they set off and travelled all day and all night, from 3.00 in the morning until 11.00 at night.
Then Daisy said, 'Mum, are both of us in your group?'
'Yes, you are,' said Daisy's mum.
Daisy was screaming in the car, going, 'Yes, yes, yes.' Then finally they got there. Daisy went, 'Summer camp.' They were so excited about it, they both put their tents up at 9.00 at night. Then Daisy and Calvin heard screaming.
They saw a little girl saying, 'They won't let me go.' Then the little girl started fading.

Daisy and Calvin ran into both of the tents, then they fell asleep. Daisy woke up in the middle of the night. She saw her mum asleep in the car. Daisy went to go and see Calvin and she couldn't see his shadow. She went and looked, there was no one there. Then Daisy slid down the hole that Calvin slid down. She saw a ghost and Calvin, they fell asleep.

Then it was morning. Their mum couldn't find where Daisy and Calvin were, then Mum saw the hole. She put a big rope down it and pulled Daisy and Calvin out, and the ghost. The ghost saw so many people that it turned into a real human, and the little girl I told you about at the beginning, turned back into a human. They all had a nice time.

Ellie Thorne (8)
St Mary Star of the Sea Catholic Primary School, St Leonards-on-sea

DOUBLE TROUBLE BEAR

One day, Hannah's teddy went for a walk when she was fast asleep. Ted found some oranges and knocked them over. He pushed over a little girl, she was really amazed that she had seen a walking teddy bear.

Hannah woke up and saw that her teddy was missing. She got dressed and asked her mum for permission to go. After breakfast, she went in search of her bear. She almost tripped over some oranges, and an angry shopkeeper was running around. Next, she saw the girl who fell over. She pointed at where Ted was hiding. He was up a tree. He came down. Ted said sorry to everyone and never went away again.

Adaeze Chikwendu (8)
St Mary Star of the Sea Catholic Primary School, St Leonards-on-sea

THE FAIRY TALE STORY

Once upon a time, King Nick and his wife, Queen Elizabeth, were having a baby girl. They named her Princess Rose. They named her Princess Rose because she liked roses and all the time she took them home.

One day, she took a little walk in the forest. When she was there, Prince Filip was riding through the forest. Princess Rose was singing to the animals, when he heard her. She only sang to them because she had no one to talk to except the animals in the forest, so she was sad. So she had another little walk in the forest with the animals and she went to her secret place, the blue river where no one else would find her except the animals. But Prince Filip knew where the blue river was. He wanted to have a nice rest, so he went, but when he got there he saw Princess Rose crying sadly.

He went over to her and said, 'Are you all right?' And he then said to her, 'Where do you live?'

She said, 'I live here, but where do you live?'

He said, 'I live in the village.'

She was surprised and she wanted to have a nice day over there to see her father, so she took him with her so he could meet her parents. They were really cross because they didn't know him, so they said to him, 'Where are your parents?'

Then they got to meet his parents and got to know them better. They left them both together.

Prince Filip said, 'Will you marry me?' and Princess Rose said yes, and they lived happily ever after.

Gabrielle Lacey (7)
St Mary Star of the Sea Catholic Primary School, St Leonards-on-sea

MR GOOGLE GHOST

On a deserted hill there lies Windborough Castle. In that castle is a googly-eyed, creepy, see-through ghost (a total weirdo). He is a thousand years old. He fought against a bloodthirsty group rebelling against the king. Mr Google Ghost haunts his killers' grave by the castle and scares anybody who comes near the castle.

One day, Charlotte and her friends decided they would go for a picnic by moonlight. They thought that the ideal place was on the hill. At 7pm they started walking the two miles to the hill.
'Let's go to the top,' said Penny, Charlotte's friend.
'Right then, let's get going,' agreed Charlotte in a bossy way.
The group climbed up the rocky sides of the hill.
'Gosh! This is hard going!' sighed Claudia.

When they reached the top, they all sat down and took deep breaths. They had been there for ten minutes and suddenly, there was a shaking of chains and a whistling sound.
'W-w-what's that noise?' shuddered Penny.
'Nothing, silly,' Charlotte told Penny.
Then Mr Google Ghost appeared and shouted, 'Who lies there? My killers have returned and I shall kill them.'
'I think we should go now,' said Claudia in a terrified voice.
As the girls ran, Mr Google Ghost swept after them. Charlotte tripped up and grazed her knee.

They still remember the day they were chased back home by Mr Google Ghost. It still lies in the girls' nightmares.

Melita Cameron-Wood (9)
St Mary Star of the Sea Catholic Primary School, St Leonards-on-sea

THE GHOST NEXT DOOR

It was night and Robert, the young boy of eight years, was asleep. Suddenly, there was a noise in the attic going *thump, thump, thump.* 'What's that noise, Eric?' Robert whispered to his brother on the other side of the room.
'I don't know, just go back to sleep.'

The next morning, Robert went up into the attic and he saw this white piece of cloth sitting in a chair reading a dusty old book which said 'How to haunt people at night'. Robert walked towards this thing. Suddenly, it looked up with its red, beaming eyes and got a knife out and slashed the air, just missing Robert, who ran and shut the attic door. You could see the knife sticking through the attic door, then it disappeared.

Eric ran and ran to his dad and dragged him to the attic and the crack in the door had gone and that was strange.
'What are you talking about Robert? There's no ghost in the attic.'
'I definitely saw a ghost in the attic chasing me.'
'You're probably just daydreaming.'

When it was dark at night, Robert heard the noise again, but it was different. *Thumpty-thump, thumpty-thump, thump, thump, thump,* went the sound. Robert darted underneath his cover and didn't come out.

The next morning, Robert got dressed and went outside to meet his friend next door. When he saw his friend, he gasped with fright, because the ghost he saw in the attic looked just like his friend. He shoved his friend in the cellar of his house and locked the door.
'You can't get out now, can you ghost?'
The ghost just walked through the cellar door. 'Robert, you just don't get it, do you? We're all ghosts except for you and you're the only one here who isn't a ghost, so you're trapped in the ghost world!'

Alexander Byott (9)
St Mary Star of the Sea Catholic Primary School, St Leonards-on-sea

THE SPOOKY HOUSE

Once upon a time there were two girls and their mother. They lived very, very happily until these people invaded their country. So the two girls had to be evacuated to the country. Strangers had to choose them and they were the last ones to be picked. It made them very nervous and they got picked by a man, and so they went to his house. It was spooky.

They took their stuff to their bedroom, then they ate and had to go to bed. They stayed awake until the man hand gone to sleep and when he went to sleep, ghosts came. So they went to the man and he said he'd send them home, but he didn't. He took them to their room and said, 'There's nothing to be afraid of, there's nothing here except your stuff and your beds.'

They heard him turn the switch off. There would still be witches and ghosts, but they went to his door, well only one of them. One stayed in the room and then the girl that was at the door of the man's room saw him press a button.

So she went in and said, 'I saw you press the button, so send me home now, OK.'

'Go home to the war and I will live. I don't care.'

So they went home, the war was finished.

Kirsten Brightiff (8)
St Mary Star of the Sea Catholic Primary School, St Leonards-on-sea

TWIN SEARCH

'Oh why, why?' wailed all the twins. They had been stick collecting and lost each other. The twins were Yasmin and Jasmine, Chloe and Soe, and Kelly and Ellie. You could never tell the difference. Anyway, let's get on with the story. Yasmin was looking for her twin, Jasmine. She saw a movement in the bushes. 'Jasmine?' she asked. But it wasn't Jasmin. 'Kelly!' she exclaimed.
'I'm not Kelly, I'm Ellie,' said Ellie. 'Anyway, have you seen her?'
'No,' said Yasmin.
'Oh,' said Ellie. 'I'll go look for her.'
'No!' Yasmin said, but she was gone.

Ellie started looking for Kelly, then she heard a rustling. 'Kelly?' asked Ellie.
'Ellie!' Kelly yelled.
Ellie went running up to her twin. 'Let's go look for the others.'
They heard Yasmin and Jasmin find each other.

Chloe was looking everywhere for Soe, then she heard a rustling up a tree! 'Soe?'
'Chloe!'
'So are you alright?'
'Yeah fine.'
'Hey, you two,' all the twins were rushing up to them, 'come on. Look, there's the cottage.'
'Mum, Mum,' said Soe.
'Yes,' said their mum. 'Yes, I can see that. Want some crumpets?'
'Yes,' they said, so they all sat down by the fire with crumpets, cookies and hot chocolate. They were very relieved for it was raining hard.

They then realised they had left Yasmin and Jasmin in the forest. 'Oh no,' they said, 'we have to go back for them.'
'Girls!' shouted their mother. 'Send Yasmin and Jasmin down!'
'Oh no, oh no.'

Evie Clifford (8)
St Mary Star of the Sea Catholic Primary School, St Leonards-on-sea

THE TREASURE HUNT

One day, Hollie, Joanna, Joanne, Madeline, Mum, Dad and I, Victoria, had a detector.

'Are we going to get some treasure?' said Madeline.

'Yes, we are going to get some treasure. I know we are going to get some treasure,' said Joanne.

'What if I find a football with metal on it?' said Joanna.

'Let me have a try on the detector,' asked Dad.

Dad found some treasure.

'Yippee!' shouted everyone.

We went home and had dinner and after that, we had a party. We played Pooh Sticks and lots of other games.

We went out again to the woods and found more treasure, and we went and found more and more. A metal football, Joanna was right. The detector was very good, because we made it that safe. That night, we went to sleep and the next morning, we went and found some more places to hunt for treasure. We found some more treasure, and more, and more, and more. We went home and put it in a box. We had finished the treasure hunt.

Victoria Cordeux (8)
St Mary Star of the Sea Catholic Primary School, St Leonards-on-sea

PLANET ZARETH

The glaze of the starry, orange sky hit Rosie and Rolf's eyes as they stepped slowly onto the planet.

'The wavy sky looks like clogs dancing,' said Rosie. 'Look at those birds!'

'Their singing is lovely and their feathers look really silky,' said Rolf.

As they walked on the grass, it seemed to grow more squelchy, until they came to a hill. They climbed it and found a door, not an ordinary door, but an orange and blue, magic door. When Rosie and Rolf tried to push and pull the door, it wouldn't budge. They tried to lift it and it worked!

They both walked through the door and saw yellow grass and purple sky, with pink and red swirls, which looked very strange but beautiful. They walked over to a tree and saw that it had something similar to pears on it. Rosie smelt them and said, 'They smell like chocolate.'

They took a bite. Rosie's tasted of a Dream Bar and Rolf's like Galaxy. They took another bite, but this time the taste and shape changed. Rosie's was like a diamond and tasted of pear, while Rolf's was a square, tasting of orange. They ate and ate until they were full up. They felt strangely sleepy, so lay down on the ground.

'Mum!' The children woke up to find their mum smiling at them. 'Mum! You'll never guess where we've been!'

Will she believe them?

Shannon Woolmer (9)
Sharps Copse Primary School, West Leigh

YOU'LL NEVER KNOW

'Mum, I'm going to bed,' I shouted. It was 10.30 and all the lights were out and everyone was asleep except me. I was thinking about my test, when I heard tapping in the loft. It sounded like it was coming down the pipework. Then I heard a voice say, 'Hey, what you doing?'

I crept out of bed and nervously walked across the landing, when an icy feeling touched my shoulder. I turned around, but nothing was there. I rushed into my mum and dad's room. I told them what I had just felt, but they wouldn't believe me. I went back into my room, terrified of the thought of what it could be.

Suddenly, I saw a black shadow. It looked like a hawk ready to pounce on its prey. I crawled across my bed and leaned up against the wall. The ghost glided over to me, his eyes shining on me. They were a deep shade of blue and they were blinding me. I cried for help, but it came out as a whisper. I shouted, 'Go away!' but it didn't listen. I shouted louder. This time it listened, but as it left, it said menacingly, 'I'll be back.'

Bradley Matthews (11)
Sharps Copse Primary School, West Leigh

A DAY IN THE LIFE OF A PEN

It was the day of the 16th of May 4065. It was a school day. First lesson, maths. I was taken from my home into the open world. Today's sums were really hard. Next is division. Division is very hard, so when will it end? 9.51. 9 minutes till English. Come on, come on.

'Time for English. Today class, we are going to do an essay about racing cars from around the world.'
What car should I do? Mclaren, Ferrari, Porsche, Fiat, Venturi, BMW, Aston Martin, TVR, Dodge Viper? I can't choose. I think I'll do a Ferrari with power steering and all the goodies.

The lesson took 30 minutes until break time. I went home and only came out after break for science. I wasn't needed for the first 30 minutes, then I started to write. It was a long piece of writing, three pages long, but in the end I did it.

It's 2.30. 40 minutes until home time. I can't wait. It's scribbler time. Anything we want to do, we can. Let's write a report. I'll do it on cars again. This time, a Mclaren F1 with airbags, V8 engine, 8 cylinders, rear boot lights and traction control system. I think a four page report should do the trick. Two pages done, soon to be finished. Three pages, three and a half, three and three quarters, finally, four. My ink's run out. Sorry, I forgot to tell you who I am. I am . . . a pen!

Darren Martin (11)
Sharps Copse Primary School, West Leigh

THE ROBOT, THE ZOMBIE AND THE FAT PEOPLE

In a town near a graveyard, there lived a flesh-eating zombie. Every week, the zombie would leave the graveyard to hunt out fat people to eat! He enjoyed chasing the fat people into the sides of buildings. Then he would eat them.

A robot had seen the zombie from a window and wanted to stop him terrorising the city. So he told his owner Ronnie, that he wanted to stop the zombie terrorising the city. Together they plotted to destroy the zombie.

The next day, Ronnie and the robot went to work on their plan. The first part of the plan was to disguise the robot with holograms to look like a skyscraper! Next, they went to visit the military base to find Major Destruction, who was their friend. They wanted to borrow a homing missile launcher. The major was confused and wanted to know why they wanted it. But after hearing about the zombie, the major was more than happy to help his friends. In fact, he gave them the special Major Destruction Missile Launcher, the powerful one on the base!

The robot was placed on a street corner, disguised with the holograms; the missile launcher was behind the robot, out of sight. Everything was ready. Ronnie had asked his fat friends to stand next to the hologram skyscraper to act as bait for the zombie. Everyone waited . . .

And waited . . . and waited!

Then just as the sun was setting and the fat people were eating cream cakes, a terrifying groan was heard. The zombie was sprinting towards the skyscraper, when suddenly, the fat people and the skyscraper disappeared, revealing the major's special missile launcher. In a flash of light, the zombie and the whole city were vaporised!

'Oops!' said the major.

Liam Holdaway (10)
West Blatchington Junior School, Hove

THE FUNNIEST TIGER

Once upon a time, there was an animal that was so funny, everyone fell apart laughing. He was so sad, because he had no one to play with him. What animal was it? OK, it was a tiger.

He was eating his lunch when he found a secret escape place and he went through it and found himself outside the zoo. He was running loose. Someone saw him in the meat shop. He ate all the meat and ran off. Then he was seen in a clothes shop, trying the clothes on. After that, he went back to the zoo and fell fast asleep.

Rhian Hart (8)
West Blatchington Junior School, Hove

THE FRIENDLY GHOST

There was a bully at school, his name was Phil. One day, Phil found Martin. Martin dared Phil to go inside the spooky castle.
'I won't go if you don't,' Phil told Martin.
'OK,' whimpered Martin, feeling very confident.

So he knocked on the castle door. There was no answer, so he walked in. All of a sudden, he heard something crying. He followed the voice. The voice came from a big room. In the corner of a bed, there was a ghost crying.
'Why are you crying?' asked Martin
'Because no one likes me,' sobbed the ghost.
'I like you,' Martin replied, grinning happily. 'Can you do me a favour?'
'Yes,' said the cheerful ghost. 'What is it?'
'There's a bully waiting outside. Can you scare him?' begged Martin.
'Of course, I'll do anything for you,' the ghost told Martin.
So it crept up behind Phil and shouted, *'Boo!'*
'Aarrgghhh!' screamed Phil. That was the end of Phil.

Ayesha Begum (8)
West Blatchington Junior School, Hove

Trouble With Red Nose Day

A little while ago in a town which was full of big green houses, there was a little red house. In this little red house, there lived the Red family. There was Daddy Red, Mummy Red, Mary Red, who was the oldest child, Mark Red, who was the middle child, then there was the baby who was called Maggie Red. They were a very happy family, until one Red Nose Day.

Red Nose Day brought a problem with the Red family. The reason it was a problem is that last year, everyone laughed at them because the Red family's noses were not brought from any shop, but their red noses were due to the fact that they all had bad colds, which made their noses very red and sore. The year before that, they'd all sold out of red noses, which meant that the Red family made their own from painted egg boxes, so you can see why they worried about Red Nose Day.

So that nobody would laugh at them this year, Maggie had decided to make sure that her family all had red noses, so every night while her family were asleep, she had painted all the red noses in the town blue, except five, which she had got her mum to buy. Well, that morning, the Red family put on the red noses and went outside to show that this year they had got it right. Or had they?

By the way, have you got your red nose? Because, don't forget, it is Red Nose day tomorrow. Yes, you got it. The Red family, which by the way are all squirrels, got the wrong day.

Amy Whelan (8)
West Blatchington Junior School, Hove

THE GHOST PIRATES

I was on my knees scrubbing the decks, when in front of me appeared the captain's wooden leg. I hastily looked up and my captain, with Polly the parrot on his shoulder, kicked my bucket over and shouted to me to scrub harder. I wasn't the only one he picked on, he also frightened Sam the cook and Silly Steven, the lookout boy.

The captain was reading a book called 'Going To War' and he thought this sounded a great idea. 'Ahoy, my maties, let's go to war with the next ship we see!' All the pirates, except me, waved their swords and cheered. Everyone got the cannonballs into the massive cannons. I carried on scrubbing the deck slowly, because I didn't want to help with the war. Silly Steven was in the crow's nest when he saw a large ship approaching.
'Ship ahoy!' shouted Steven.
All the others got ready to fire the cannons. Our pirate's flag should have warned them that we were bloodthirsty men, ready for action, but they just seemed to get closer. Captain ordered the cannons to be fired and they left our ship with a loud bang.

The balls just went through the ship and before we knew it, the ship went through us. We looked at each other in amazement, but then we should have known as we are all ghosts. Captain shouted, 'Let's return to our watery graves until another ship sails through our waters.'

Lucy Bone (8)
West Blatchington Junior School, Hove

A Day In The Life Of David Beckham

Today I woke up at 10.10am in the morning, quite early for such a good footballer like myself. The only problem was, I woke up in hospital. I had nurses near my precious thumb, with plaster and bandages all around me. I remembered that I had been taken off the pitch after the witch doctor put the curse on me.

The only reason we won was because I was on the pitch. I am so missing my delicate Victoria and my dear children, Brooklyn and Romeo. After my bandages come off, I am going out walking with my new sunglasses and showing off my football skills to Sven.

Now that I have told you the things that I am going to do after I have got the bandages off my thumb, why don't we talk about things that I can do? Like lunch! I am starving, let's go to the café. Oops, nearly forgot my sunglasses! Right, I'm ordering, a chicken, cheese and mayo sandwich and a bottle of Lucozade please. Scrummy! I loved the company I had for lunch. Now why don't we go shopping for new boots, football boots of course.

Don't be distracted by me writing my autographs. Right, I think Victoria mentioned this shop, let's go in. Quick, look over here, there's a smashing pair of boots. Let me try them on. They look super, especially with my plaited hair. I think I will buy this pair of boots.

Right, let's go and get dinner, all this shopping has made me feel hungry. I am having chicken soup with brown bread and butter for dinner. Delicious! I love that.

Now I am going to practise my footie skills, train for August. Bye, lovely company. Ta-ta.

Shannon Brown (9)
West Blatchington Junior School, Hove

A DAY IN THE LIFE OF A LION

I woke up this morning with the sun blazing down on my face. My cubs were playing tag already. I lifted my head to get up when I saw a zebra, standing all on its own, in the shade of an old oak tree.

'Shhh, be quiet!' I growled at my cubs. I slunk into the tall grass. The zebra's eyes were twitching vigorously. He bent his head to chew on some fresh, green grass as I got closer. I leapt and caught it by the neck. I held on as tightly as I could. As I lay on the floor, I called to my cubs. They bounded over and tucked in.

By the way my name is Leone the lion. My cubs' names are Tootsey and Oakley. Tootsey is a little girl and is 12 weeks old. Oakley is the oldest and loves climbing trees. (That's why I called him Oakley!)

The zebra tasted lovely and I hid it in a bush for dinner. For the rest of the day I lazed in the sun, watching over my cubs while they played tag again.

At dinner time I got the zebra out of the bush and called my cubs. They ripped the remaining meat from the carcass and gulped it down. I ate what was left and left the skeleton to rot.

The day was easy and I hoped that it would be the same tomorrow, as I snuggled down with my cubs to go to sleep.

Megan Hogan (10)
West Blatchington Junior School, Hove

A DAY IN THE LIFE OF BUFFY THE VAMPIRE SLAYER

Hi, my name is Buffy. My real name is Sarah Michelle Gellar. Today I woke up in LA. I am meant to be dyeing my hair blonde but the director said I had to be in the new movie of Scooby-Doo. I am playing Daphne, it's so weird. Anyway I had a really funny letter from one of my fans, I think it was a girl. She said her brother's birthday was on the same day as my birthday, the 14th April. By the way I just read some of my letters, not all of them (sorry for any inconvenience).

I totally hate it when I have to kiss Spike's lips. I feel really sorry for Willow and Tara when they have to kiss each other, it's totally sick, nobody else has to.

I will send some chocolates to the funniest letters.

Sadia Atmani (9)
West Blatchington Junior School, Hove

JIMMY'S ADVENTURE

'Yo, my name is Jim, short for Jimmy. I'm a hamster, a Russian dwarf. I like to eat nuts, lots of them.

One day I got out of my cage. I climbed out of the cage door. 'I'm free, I'm free!' I yelled. What adventure should I go on? I know, I'll go swimming in the sink! I'll use up lots of my energy and turn on the tap. I did it! The soap was the diving board. I love to splash about in the house.

Someone came into the kitchen and unplugged the sink. Jim was quickly swirling around and going down the drain. Thank goodness he didn't go down.

Jimmy thought, *I've had enough adventure for one day,* so he crawled back into his cage and cuddled up with his teddy bear and never tried to escape again.

Lilli Petrosian (9)
West Blatchington Junior School, Hove

A DAY IN THE LIFE OF BUFFY THE VAMPIRE SLAYER

Buffy's *the Slayer* who slays monsters with her Watcher, Giles and *The Scooby Gang's* help. The members are Willow and Tara who are Wiccas in love. Xander and Anya are in love. Spike is a vampire and Dawn is Buffy's sister. Dawn was once the key to a portal, which unleashed Hell. Glory, a god, wanted Dawn. She searched for her and found her. She made Dawn's blood open the portal. Dawn was going to jump to close it, but Buffy stopped her. Dawn was *made* from Buffy. Buffy could also jump. Buffy jumped and died. Her friends thought she was in Hell so Willow brought her back.

Buffy was patrolling, looking for a demon called The Judge. They had been searching for him. An old book said no weapon forged could destroy him - but that was then! Giles realised a rocket launcher would kill him.

Suddenly Buffy heard roaring. The Judge appeared and ran to Buffy. She kicked him, he scratched her face.
'Now I'm mad!' Buffy said. She kicked his nose and he fell in pain.
'Giles, *now!*'
Giles jumped from behind a tomb holding a rocket launcher. Everyone else appeared holding jars. The Judge jumped up, Spike and Giles shot the rocket at him. It hit him and his body pieces flew everywhere. The gang collected the parts into jars.
'Make sure you get every piece,' shouted Giles, 'or he'll be back.'
The group cheered that he'd died and went home.
But there was one piece left!

Ellen Hodgkins (9)
West Blatchington Junior School, Hove

A DAY IN THE LIFE OF A PIECE OF PAPER

I ran down the stairs as fast as I could, I was so hungry. I knew there was still an apple left. I made myself a hot, delicious cup of blistering tea. I took one sip and *boom!* I had turned into a piece of paper! I had been picked up by a googly, huge piece of hand. I felt the black tickling thing on me that gave me a major fright. After that I looked down on myself and saw some still tickling squiggly things. The only thing that I could read was *The family's biggest secret!* I will always remember that message. I sat there in so much horror.

It's the spring festival today and I want to go but I can't because I'm a piece of paper, I thought. All of a sudden - *ssswooosh!* I had been blown onto a table in the spring festival hall. A girl went over to get a cup of tea, she put it on the table and accidentally knocked it over on me.

All of a sudden, *boom!* I had turned back into a human!

Sophie Cooper (8)
Whitchurch CE Primary School, Whitchurch

A Day In The Life Of A . . .

I glide through the clouds looking down at the view. Full of pride in the sky, I feel I should boast and say, 'Look at me I'm flying!' I land at my children's feet, feeding them. I have busy days being chased by birds like eagles, they try and catch me. But I feel happy to go wherever I like and I mean wherever!

My wingspan is like the propellers on an aeroplane. Cats are a big threat to my family. My children, three girls and three boys, have to fly away because the cat tries to catch us. We have to fly away as far as we can from that mean old beast. We enjoy flying, but not from animals that chase us.

I heard a bell ringing in my ear. I looked down and people were throwing stones. I felt scared, shuffling with my children, moving and they were okay. Feeling like a stunt man, I drifted to the nest, forgetting about the mean cat.

My children can fly. They went away and I felt lonely but happy with less on my mind. I love my children and hopefully next year I will have some more.

Have you guessed what I am yet?

Lydia Hopkins (8)
Whitchurch CE Primary School, Whitchurch

A DAY IN THE LIFE OF A MOUSE

7pm
As I opened my eyes, the first thing I saw was four furry paws, prowling slowly and endlessly across my front door. There was cheese in the kitchen, how was I supposed to get it with that cat about? I rather wanted it for breakfast!

8.57pm
I was almost going to give up on getting the cheese when the cat was called. Hooray!

9.01pm
Great. Just great. The only reason he was being called was to say goodnight to the humans. He only took four minutes. At least they're going to bed.

9.32pm
I watched the cat as soon as he came back into the room. He disappeared! I crept out of my hole. Then he came back. I had to dive back in again. I could still smell the cheese.

10.46pm
The cat went outside. I heard the cat flap slam. It was safe for me to come out. I scurried up the curtain and peered out the window. The cat was in the field outside. I crept down the curtain. I had no idea where the kitchen was.

11.46pm
It took me an hour to scurry up and down the curtains to find the kitchen. I squeezed under the door.

11.51pm
I started to get excited. I could see the cheese! I sat, mesmerised. Then I pinched it. The cat ruined everything and saw me. I had to squeeze under the door with the cheese.

12.01am
The thing I needed most in the world was help. Why didn't I move? Even worse, it took me a while to find my front door!

1.03am

The humans woke. Thank heavens! Not surprising. I did make a lot of noise.

1.14am

I was never going through that again for cheese. I knew it was early to be going to bed but I was exhausted.

Katrina Drayton (9)
Whitchurch CE Primary School, Whitchurch

A DAY IN THE LIFE OF A TENNIS RACQUET

There I was lying at the front of the shop, when some sort of mammal picks me up and takes me away. The mammal pulled a key out of a pocket on its leg, opened a door and he entered. Then he started practising tennis with me. Then at about 4 o'clock, I found out that the person was called Tim Henman and he was going to use me to go against Gregory Smith.

I noticed that every time Tim hit the ball I felt a sharp pain jolt up my handle. Tim was very lucky and won the match by five points. In the next hour we were in another match and it started. Everyone cheered when Tim scored, but we were behind by ten points. Then Tim made up a strategy for himself and walked on court. Tim ran like the wind and hit the ball and it flew through the air like a jet and . . . we won.

Oliver Flawith (8)
Whitchurch CE Primary School, Whitchurch

A DAY OF A LIFETIME AS A LAMB

Early one morning I woke up in lovely fresh, green grass, but how? Oh I remember, the farmer moved us into another field because the last one got all smelly and horrible.

For breakfast I had some grass, it was so delicious I couldn't stop eating. Finally I stopped and decided to take a little rest. *Baa, baa!* My mum's bleating woke me up. She wanted me to do my stretches. I felt so tired and sighed, but had to do them anyway. Up, down, up, up, down. Straight after, I had to take medicine.

'Come sheep,' said the farmer in his cranky voice. It was my turn. I stepped forward to take my medicine. I thought he must be crazy putting that thing in my mouth. My mum kept nudging me to move a little closer to the farmer! Then that's when it happened, that killing machine went into my mouth and felt like it was sticking into my tongue. That's when it started to get nasty; I kicked the farmer and ran for my life. I spotted a barn and ran into it and settled down and got cosy.

Later, my tummy felt a bit funny and before I knew it, I was sick, *everywhere! Yes it was the medicine,* I thought, or maybe it was the running straight after having it. Then I saw the farmer staring straight at me. He came over and got a creamy white blanket and laid it over me. Then I knew the medicine was harmless. He carried me back where we all lay in the barn asleep.

Chloe Kelley (8)
Whitchurch CE Primary School, Whitchurch

A Day In The Life Of Mimmy, The Cat

As I sit on the bed, I remember the day that I went out to show the others who was the queen of cats. I already had it planned. I would bite one cat, stick my paw in another cat, scratch the third cat and bend the last one's ear.

I went outside, but the only cat there was a cat I had never seen before. As I looked closer, I realised that she was smiling at me! Her smile said, 'Hi, I'm Kitty.' So I smiled back as if to say, 'Hi! I'm Mimmy.'

We went to catch some mice, but ended up bumping into the other cats. Kitty and I just turned round and strutted home. Kitty came round and we formed the 'Secrets' club. We told each other secrets and Kitty got out a book. She turned to a page and showed me a paragraph. The title was 'Relatives Of Mimmy The Cat'. I stared at the paper and was surprised to see the name 'Kitty' at the bottom of the cousins list. I stared at Kitty and gave her a look that said, 'Why didn't you tell me?'
'I wanted to find out how well we got on first,' was the look that came. Then we had a midnight feast and went to sleep.

Elysia Oakham (8)
Whitchurch CE Primary School, Whitchurch

A DAY IN THE LIFE OF STEVEN GERRARD

7am to 9am

I woke up calmly, feeling nervous. I was playing in the Worthington Cup final in Cardiff. Changing into a grey Nike top, black Nike shorts and white Nike trainers, I went downstairs to have breakfast. I wasn't as anxious now. I made a boiled egg, it couldn't get any better. Soon after breakfast, I packed my Liverpool training kit. Just before nine o'clock, I travelled to Cardiff by the team coach.

9am to 1pm

The team practised dribbling, passing, shooting, tackling and sprinting. After an hour, we had our team talk and everyone was very fidgety, as our manager chose our line up. I was playing in centre midfield and was hoping to score the winner. I could feel I was going to score a cracker to win the cup. We went onto the pitch to do some more training for half an hour and then went inside to get changed into our kit. I wore number seventeen on our home shirt.

3pm to 5pm

Out we came, hoping for victory. Michael and I kicked off, but I was quickly tackled by Beckham. Later in the game, Diddi got the ball, he passed to me and I shot and scored! With ten minutes to go, I passed to Michael who ran up field and scored our second goal. We had won the cup. I got home and went to bed after an exhausting day.

Jack Allen (8)
Whitchurch CE Primary School, Whitchurch

A Day In The Life Of David Beckham

I was lying in bed fast asleep. Suddenly, out of nowhere, the alarm rang. I slowly got out of bed, putting my suit on, along with my gold Rolex, and ran downstairs.

Outside was the Manchester United team bus. I walked up the steps waving goodbye, sat down with the Nevilles, who were later joined by Rio Ferdinand.

We were on the outskirts of Upton Park where we would play the biggest match of the season - West Ham United. I slowly walked up the glistening silver steps into the changing room and got changed into my Nike tracksuit and walked onto the pitch for our warm up.

Returning back down the tunnel after the warm up, I gently pulled on my number 7 shirt. I laced my white boots and the manager came over to me and handed me the armband. I gasped, tension was building, what would happen?

I was on the pitch standing in the centre circle, ready to shake the hand of the West Ham captain. We shook hands vigorously. The referee flipped the coin, we had won kick-off.

Van Nistelrooy received the ball from Scholes and hacked the ball up-field to me. I ran, then I was fouled and the opposing player got sent off. As I placed the ball on the muddy pitch, thousands of thoughts ran through my head. I stepped up and smacked the ball home. My teammates jumped on me - I had won the game.

Jack Oxford (9)
Whitchurch CE Primary School, Whitchurch

A DAY IN THE LIFE OF KAT SLATER

In the morning when I wake up, I go downstairs, whack a bit of jam on my warm toast then drink my tea, alone in my cosy sitting room. After that, I go upstairs and have a bubbly bath with soap, then get dressed. Next, I go to wash up the plates and that, and next I go to work as a barmaid at the Queen Victoria. Walking over, five minutes it took - not that far at all.

When I arrived at the door, I walked straight in. I went straight to work with Alfie, that's all. I had served about 15 customers already, when the evening drew on. I was sat on a stool waiting for some customers when the phone rang. *Ring, ring.* It was for me. I had been invited to Angie's Den, so I checked with Alfie and of course he said yes, and I walked over. I had a great time with my three sisters. Then later on, I walked home and I laid on my bed and slept till the sun came up from behind the dark and gloomy clouds.

Chantelle Hardy (9)
Whitchurch CE Primary School, Whitchurch

A DAY IN THE LIFE OF MY DOG FAITH

As I lie in my owner's comfy bed with my best friend, Shadow, by my side, there are bones dancing in my mind because I am so hungry and my tummy is rumbling. I just can't wait until my owner gets up to give me and Shadow our breakfast. After a long wait, he gets up and goes downstairs. Me and Shadow follow at fast pace.

When we reach the warm kitchen, he gives us our food then lets us out in our back garden. Shadow challenges me to a game of rough play-fighting and I gladly accept. I beat him with attitude.
I go to take a nap on our mats by the window for about two hours.

At lunchtime I can smell a delicious meal. As I follow the smell that is surrounding me, into the kitchen, my eyes fall upon a scrumptious plate of roast chicken. I quickly glance around, and when I am sure that nobody is looking, I sneak under the table. There is not much space so I have to be careful.

When all our bellies are full, we watch a DVD. As I put my head on the comfy ground, my eyes fall into a quiet sleep.

Alana Webb (9)
Whitchurch CE Primary School, Whitchurch

THE LUCKY SURVIVAL OF HOMER SIMPSON

In the morning, all I do is sleep . . . sleep . . . sleep, and after what seems like centuries of sleep, I get dressed, but today it took a whole hour! When I reached down for my trousers, I ripped my pants, bellowed a massive, *'D'oh!'* and got changed into some other underwear. I put my trousers on again and when I reached down for my T-shirt and put it on, little did I know that I had ripped my trousers. I knew I was going to be late, so I skipped breakfast, grabbed my lunchbox and scrambled into the car. Once inside, I scoffed my lunch as quickly as possible because it was midday by now, as I took an hour to get dressed.

When I reached my work, I walked one step inside and I heard my boss saying, 'Simpson, why are you an hour late? And what's that rip in your trousers?'
'Rip . . . ? Trousers?' I said, embarrassed.
'You're fired!' roared my boss, Monty Burns.
'D'oh!' I blasted out, then strolled to Moe's.

I ended up getting drunk on beer and I accidentally ran off a cliff. I landed on my stomach, bounced back up and flew all the way across Springfield. I broke my legs when I fell through the roof of my house. But this time I blurted out, *'Woo-hoo!'* because the first thing that came into my mind was that I could have breakfast in bed every morning.

Dayle Franklin (9)
Whitchurch CE Primary School, Whitchurch

A DAY IN THE LIFE OF A KEBAB

As I sit there, the light penetrating my skin, I feel that something is missing, like a part of me! 'Are my onions missing?'

As I sit there wondering, a butcher comes up to me and he starts looking me in the olives, as if I was some kind of unidentifiable frying object. He puts me in a bag with these friends, the peppers and mushrooms. What's he doing? 'Hey, I'm going to suffocate.' He could not hear me. I couldn't hear what he was saying.
'. . . a worthless piece of meat for baking.'
He hands me over to a lady, I was stuffed in a stuffy environment. 'Where is she going?'

As soon as she stopped, there was a glance of gleaming light, was this the end? As she makes her way to the white shelf full of other things, she rams me onto it. She leaves me to simmer in my new, cold environment. She takes me out and lays me on a piece of wood and pulls out a knife. She lays me on a grill and covers me in silver foil. It was getting hot, later I was crisp under my silver sheet. She uncovers me and puts me on a plate.

'Was this my ending, was this my new home?' As I softly slide down a cave with stale air, it goes dark, I can't see. 'I guess this must be it.'

Sam Bridgeman (9)
Whitchurch CE Primary School, Whitchurch

A DAY IN THE LIFE OF . . . ?

As I stood on the freshly-mowed Oval, I shouted to Giles, 'Go and bowl.' As Giles stepped up, it span into the wicket. *Boom!* 'Catch,' I shouted. Hoggard ran and ran and then . . . he, he dropped it. 'Darn it!' I cried. That over was a massive let down.

The whole innings went pretty much the same way until . . . James Anderson came to bowl.

The next over I could not describe, I was stunned! Every time the ball hit the stumps (that was often) it was like a rocket getting speeding tickets on the way to orbit, a javelin being thrown to infinity, or a ball hoofed to Pluto and back. The score now was 575-10 *all out!*

That was my day in the life of someone who is a cricketer, plays for England, and his name begins with N.

James Halle-Smith (8)
Whitchurch CE Primary School, Whitchurch

A Day In The Life Of David Beckham's Favourite Football Boots

I stepped up, heaving my whole body at the ball. I waited, watching as the ball went tumbling high in the air. It curled and was heading for the crossbar, but . . . just before I gave up, it dunked right into the net. We had equalised in the last minute, things were looking good, a corner to us. Beckham took it. With me clinging to his foot, we were sure to score. David crossed it and Roy Keane smashed it on his left foot and scored! What a goal! The team celebrated. The referee blew this whistle for full-time. All the players ran into the changing rooms in delight.

When we got home, I was polished and put amongst Beckham's other boots. I thought I was the luckiest pair of boots in the world, I was David Beckham's favourite football boots. I could tell I was, because he always picked me to play in the matches and I had Brooklyn printed on the left boot and Romeo printed on the right.

As I stared at the other boots, I thought about my times in the Adidas sport shop, the pleasant smell of new design boots being made. Then something made me stop. What was this? Then I saw it. It disgusted me! There, clinging to his arms, were some brand new football boots! What would I do? I wouldn't be Beckham's best boots any more. The other boots started bullying me, causing my perfectly-sewed leather to snap in half. I was broken!

George Mathias (8)
Whitchurch CE Primary School, Whitchurch

A Day In The Life Of A Champions League Football

I was perched in my yellow net with all the other balls, as normal. It was *so* boring just sitting in a bag, waiting for someone to kick you. It's not very pleasant being kicked by someone all the stupid time, is it? I mean, if you were a ball and you were being kicked, you wouldn't like it, would you? I don't really think so. There's one time I wouldn't mind being kicked. That's the Champions League final. I've always wished to be in the Berkshire Balls News. Especially because whoever is the first ball to play in the final, will be the thousandth ball to be in the news.

I heaved myself out of the bag, because the final was at Cardiff and I was on the western side of Berkshire, so I had to travel a long way. Bounce, bounce, bounce, I went. Bounce, over the fence.

Suddenly, I halted. What was it? It read *'Compass'*. A compass?
'You want to know what a compass is, eh?' a voice shrieked from above. I rolled over to see who it was. It was a carrion crow.
'Yes please,' I said, politely.
'It's a thing that tells you where you're going.'
'Well, thank you.' So I bounced along again.

Two hours later, I got to the Cardiff stadium. I revolved into the stadium under the crowd. Suddenly, someone picked me up and ran onto the pitch. I was the ball to be in the final. I was the ball . . .

David Eves (8)
Whitchurch CE Primary School, Whitchurch

A DAY IN THE LIFE OF . . .

As I woke sleepily, I swam to the top of my tank, waiting for my keeper to feed me. Mmm, lovely. The strong scent of fish filled the sanctuary. I had to do loads of tricks to be awarded breakfast, like jumping through hoops, swimming and diving, and after breakfast I just had to carry on as the seats filled up.

Soon it was lunchtime and groups of children came over to feed me. I got the largest breakfast (because I did the best tricks). A little girl toddled over with a huge fish in her hand. She tried to give it to me, but I was too far away and she fell in. I slid my wet body under her to break her fall, but she couldn't balance, so I bit her dress before she was under too deep. I gently and quickly pulled her to the surface, worrying I would rip her clothes, but I didn't and when I reached the surface the keeper was there to congratulate me on my performance.

The wet, uncomfortable girl went home with her parents and I was given the big fish and it was definitely worth it. It was lovely, and I also got a medal which my keeper looked after whilst I played.

Martha Robinson (8)
Whitchurch CE Primary School, Whitchurch

A Day In The Life Of The Dove Of peace

I slowly opened my eyes and saw I was perched up in a tree and I yawned loudly. I saw a worm. I quickly soared down to pick it up with my beak. I trapped it in my beak and flew back to my tree to eat it. A couple of hours later, I saw an old lady standing there with a note. I thought to myself, *she probably wants me to take it to someone.* As I flew down to her, I took it, it said the name: To The Dove Of Peace. I opened it, it was some sort of invite. I dropped the note and flew back to my tree.

It's midday and I am eating lunch. I thought to myself and I was lonely. *I know what will cheer me up, I will lay some eggs,* I thought excitedly. I was sitting there for hours and hours and suddenly, two eggs popped out!

I've just got to keep them warm, I thought. I was sitting there for six hours. The eggs were hatching and one little dove popped out, an hour later. the second dove popped out! I sat there admiring my children. I sat them in my nest and I flew off to find some insects.

I came back and gave them the worm I found. I watched them split the worm in two, then they ate the worm. I put them to bed. I watched them doze off, so I went to bed and got some sleep.

Hollie Varndell (9)
Whitchurch CE Primary School, Whitchurch

A DAY IN THE LIFE OF A FOOTBALL

The day had come for me, I was going to be the most important ball of all. The World Cup Final was only *two hours away.* I could feel the tension, it was unbearable. I saw a man come into the warm room. He came and picked me up, I felt really proud. Kick-off was in ten minutes.

The players came onto the pitch. They went to the centre spot and had a coin toss. Spain had won. I was put on the centre spot and off they went. I got smacked up-field, Brazil picked me up and passed me to Ronaldo. Ronaldo smacked me against the crossbar. By the half-hour mark, I was bruised and I had a pounding headache. When half-time came, I was glad.

Before I knew it, I was back on the pitch. After 50 minutes, Raul had won a free kick, so he ran up and curled me into the goal. I scored a goal. The rest of the second half flew by. It was the 90th minute, the tension was better than ever and suddenly the whistle went. I couldn't believe it, I had scored. I might have been battered, but I had been part of the *World Cup Final.* I was so proud of myself, I was part of it.

Alex Rudge (9)
Whitchurch CE Primary School, Whitchurch

A Day In The Life Of A . . . ?

I woke up suddenly, got dressed quickly and went downstairs to find my breakfast. It was there as usual on my own little table in the dining room. Breakfast was bacon, eggs, sausage and beans. I was just about to start eating when I heard some strange giggles and somebody saying, 'Whatever is she doing?' As soon as I heard this, I immediately put down my knife and fork.

I could hear my mum saying something about having a new toy. She seemed to be feeding me, but it wasn't with bacon and eggs. She was putting my worst CD in, called 'How To Use A Dictionary'. Why was this happening to me? What had happened to me? Things improved a little when she put my favourite DVD in.

When the film was over and done with, Mum went back to my desktop, a colourful butterfly filled the screen. Its colours were all the colours of the rainbow, it was gorgeous. There were trees all around it, with bright green leaves lying on the bright yellow fields.

When my mum left the dining room, something awful happened. The smiling face on the screen turned sad, a bomb appeared and there was a *bang* from where I was sitting. My mum ran in and asked me why I had thrown my breakfast on the floor, saying what a naughty . . . I was.

Alice Buckley (9)
Whitchurch CE Primary School, Whitchurch

A DAY IN THE LIFE OF A HORSE

I stood in my bed of shavings waiting for my owner to come and get me my breakfast and take me into the field with all that delicious grass. I had about half an hour in the paddock. After that, I went for a schooling session. I had at least ten of them. After that, I went to see my friends grazing away in the field. My owner said I couldn't go back into the field because we were just about to go for a ride from the stable around the village.

My owner tacked me up at the stable and then we went around the village. We went past the school, around the pond, across the creaky bridge and back into the yard, then in to where my stable is, where my owner untacked me and took me into the field for the night. Most of the horses stay in the field all night. Anyway, it's easier for me because I get so hungry cantering and trotting around the schools. I can also get more water in the field. I love playing around with my mates, Ziggy and Odette. I've only been out for a while because about a month ago, another horse kicked me and I had a nasty cut on my leg. I played for a bit and then went to sleep.

Callie Newman (9)
Whitchurch CE Primary School, Whitchurch

A DISASTER IN THE MAKING

We are being filmed for children everywhere to watch. As soon as I get up, I have to wake the colony. So I got up and called the colony together. I told them we were being filmed so they had to find food.

One ant hour later, the leading soldier ant found a human picnic. I decided that as we were being filmed, we had to make the most of it, so I stole a packet of sugar and a chocolate bar. But this wasn't enough so some soldier ants stole a jam doughnut. The camera crew asked if we could take one more thing, so the worker ants took some ice cream and sweets.

After we had done this, I decided that we should go home. The only problem was that to get home, we had to cross the sea. I told my ants we had to make a boat and get home before dark. As I began to take them across the sea, a wave came and some ants were drowned. I struggled home with what was left of the colony.

I thought things couldn't get any worse, but we met a dog. When we finally got home, we had lost all the food. Things just couldn't get any worse!

Now we have to eat yesterday's leftovers. That is not good, but at least we have something.

A human is coming and is pouring boiling water over us. What will happen now?

Charlotte Langston (9)
Whitchurch CE Primary School, Whitchurch

A DAY IN THE LIFE OF A STRAY DOG

I woke up to find myself on a heap of grass in a massive garden. I got up onto my feet. Little did I know a huge house was awaiting me. I could just about see the opening of a huge porch. I continued to walk down the stony path and crept inside the door, and then I saw the most distinguished lady. She was walking down a thick red carpet. I jumped up and she held me in her arms and she stroked me. At first, it was weird, but then I got used to it. I felt happy and relaxed.

She put me down and let me explore. I happily walked up the stairs and found a comfortable spot and started to fall asleep, my eyes were heavy and I was very tired. I had a funny dream, but it came to a strange ending.

I went out for an early morning walk. I noticed people were cheering, 'Queen, Queen, Queen!' I realised who she was. No wonder she had a big and beautiful house. She was the Queen and I was her dog! At last I had found a home. I would never have to go searching again.

Emma Matland (9)
Whitchurch CE Primary School, Whitchurch

A DAY IN THE LIFE OF MISS CHRISTOPHERSON

There I stood, ready for work, thinking I was a special teacher. I set off to my pupils who were patiently waiting. I eventually arrived. I read the register out. We swapped for literacy. By the end of literacy, I had loads of work to mark. I was like, *oh no, I will never be able to get through these.*

Then we swapped for numeracy and by the end of numeracy, I had another pile of books to mark. Now I was panicking. Next, we had science and by the end of science, I had another pile of work to mark. By the end of the day, I had about ninety books to mark.

At the end of the day, I sat in my hot, stuffy classroom marking the books, thinking, *why am I in the classroom instead of the beach?* I thought I was just going to collapse, but luckily I managed to mark all ninety books.

Even though it's hard work, it's fun, because I get to teach different children and because they are learning. If I did not teach, the children would not learn, because there would be one teacher less in the school.

So I went to my car and drove home because I'd had a hard day at school. When I got home, I went to bed.

Gemma Freeborough (9)
Whitchurch CE Primary School, Whitchurch

A DAY IN THE LIFE OF A . . .

Suddenly I woke up. There was this horrible miaowing sound ringing in my ears. I looked around quickly with my small, round, black eyes. My feathers stood on end. My ears were on stalks and I realised that the horrible sound must be a cat and it was coming after me! As fast as my wings could take me, I went off to warn my friends.

I got there as quick as a flash and we all went racing off with our wings flapping like mad. Finally, we were able to come home again, but I was sure that the cat was hiding somewhere. To my horror, the cat was actually climbing our tree. It was nearly up to us, so we dived out of our nest and started to fly down over the pond to escape from the cat. The cat tried to follow us, but didn't notice the pond.

Splash! In he fell.

We were safe at last. It was time to find some lunch, so we flew off to the end of our garden and found some juicy worms to eat. When we got back to our tree, the cat was coming out of the pond and looked very sorry for himself. We played some of our favourite games until finally it was time to go to bed.

A typical day in the life of a . . . *bird!*

Emma Clark (7)
Whitchurch CE Primary School, Whitchurch

A DAY IN THE LIFE OF A SPECIAL HORSE

I awoke early in the morning, the grass underneath me had frost on it. I got up and started to lick the fresh water off the soft blades of grass. I heard the gate click and looked up. It was one of my owner's helpers. The old lady who owned me often rode me through crowds of people - it was all so weird!

She came up to me and led me away to the stables, and got a brush and started to groom my fur. I ate hay while she groomed me. When she'd finished, she led me out into the yard, put a saddle on me and reins, then she started to plait my mane, and she pulled it tight. I whinnied a bit, but she soon finished. I looked up at the scorching hot sun.
'Come on, Honey.' The lady led me to the mounting block.
'She's ready,' she shouted.

The old lady carefully walked out of the building and up to the block. She got up and got onto my back (as she did, she sighed in relief). The old lady nudged me to walk.

About an hour later, we were in the centre of London. There were crowds of people rushing about, cheering, clapping. Suddenly I saw something. It said, 'Queen' in big letters! Suddenly I figured something out. The old lady wasn't just an old lady - she was the Queen and I was her horse!

Kate Beer (9)
Whitchurch CE Primary School, Whitchurch

A DAY IN THE LIFE OF A FISH CALLED JULES

I slowly woke up and went for a quick swim. When I was having a swim, I thought today would be a lovely day with the river flowing gently. Then I went to the top of the river to get ready for the tennis match (Tim Henman v Gregory Smith). I watched very carefully and finally the match had ended and Tim Henman won!

Then I noticed how pretty the sky was. There were no clouds in sight. Then I swam gracefully down to the bottom of the river. At least I tried to, but my fin was caught in something. It was sharp, but not too sharp, but I still couldn't get it off! Then I realised that my fin was caught in a *fishing rod*. I thought, *don't panic now,* but I did!

The next thing I remember is swimming into a big tank. After a while, this kind of mammal put her face right up to mine. Then another mammal picked me up gently and put me in a see-through bag (it was like being poured in a kettle).

The next thing I remember is swimming into a small, but cosy tank. I remembered the times with my old owner. He was caring, loving, and never forgot my food. (He put me back in the river.) But then I suppose Tim Henman doesn't want a fish. Tim Henman didn't give me a name either, but I was never comfortable in the old tank. This owner gave me a name, it was Jules - and this tank was perfect!

Isabelle Crome (8)
Whitchurch CE Primary School, Whitchurch

A DAY IN THE LIFE OF A RED ANT

As I grasp onto my lovely layer of skin, I remember my days on the ant hill where the rest of my family are hiding. The sun beats down on me as I am its victim, just lying there waiting to die. The landscape of skin was annoying me. I crawl around thinking what to do next.

I climb down from the bleeding skin and I come across this grey material. What could it be? Could it be a cloak, or could it be shorts, or could it be trousers? As I climb down, I think what will the ant hill look like when I get back?

When I got back, my mum and dad were not to be seen. Where were they? I searched for my mum and dad. *Suddenly,* a giant flying doo-doo thing flew right past me. Then it came darting back, right at me. It nearly killed me.

I sprinted as fast as I could in search for a hole. Then suddenly from out of the mist, I saw a hole. I headed in its direction, then dived into it. My mum and dad were sitting there and we lived happily ever after.

Jordan England (7)
Whitchurch CE Primary School, Whitchurch

A DAY IN THE LIFE OF A KITTEN

As I open my eyes for the first time today, I feel four warm sausages sliding under my tummy. The sausages lift me up into the air and I find myself staring into the face of a giant. The giant had long yellow hair and blue eyes - then she carefully deposited me into a cat carrier and shut the lid. As I bumped along in the carrier, I feared for my immediate future.

'Have you got it?' called a high-pitched voice from an open window.
'Yes I have, it's a boy,' replied the long-haired giant. 'Here he is!' added the giant, throwing open the door.

Inside there is a smaller giant who looks like a miniature form of the yellow-haired one.
'Oh, he's so cute - what shall we call him?' asked the little one.
'Let's decide later, but right now, we need to get home,' said the big one. Now she's getting into the front seat and a horrible noise pollutes the air.

About half an hour later, the little one said something. 'I think we should call him Tyrant - because he's ginger.'
'OK dear, if you want, he's your kitten after all,' said the big one.
As this conversation is going on, I am sitting here wondering what has happened to my brothers and sisters.

About two hours later, we are still driving. I stop thinking about my brothers and sisters and turned my attention to the birds flying past the window - someday I'm going to catch one of them.

Guess what happens next?

Guy Niblett (9)
Whitchurch CE Primary School, Whitchurch

THE TRAGIC DEATH OF HOMER SIMPSON

'Homer, wake up,' said Marge.
'What? Where's the doughnuts?' Homer said.
'You're going to be late for work.'
'Nooo,' Homer said.
'Why can't I get these?'
'Bart get out of here,' Homer said. 'Bart, who's that?'
'Nelson.'
'D'oh. See you later,' Homer said.
Errrrnnk.

'D'oh,' Homer said. 'Hey, that's Lenny's car, I didn't know they were here.'
'Hello Mr Burns,' Homer said.
'What's that rip in your trousers?' he said
'What rip? I thought . . . d'oh!' Homer said.
'You're fired,' he said.

An hour later, Homer went to Moe's. He bought eighteen Duff beers. Homer knew this would probably kill him, but he didn't care. Homer was on his last beer but he was running towards the bridge, when the bridge opened with Homer on it. Homer banged his head, fell in the river and sank.

Luckily, there was a helicopter nearby, but it could hardly pick him up. They came crashing down and the helicopter set Homer's clothes on fire. Homer jumped into the river, sank and drowned.

Adam Hopgood (9)
Whitchurch CE Primary School, Whitchurch

THE LONELY GIRL

Once there was a girl, a very lonely girl. She had been attached to strings the whole of her life. All she wanted to do was get away from everything and everyone. Her life was even harder when it came down to work. She was pulled left to right and up and down.

One day she got so bored she nearly died through boredom. She eventually got to do something and guess what it was? Even more work in the puppet show. She was poked to speak, and ordered around like an army soldier.

She got so annoyed with being ordered to speak; she didn't want to do it anymore. Once she got sick, but she still had to do it, in spite of being so ill.

That night she had one wish and wished to get down from the strings. In the morning, she was gone . . . *but no one knows where!*

Shanice Horn (11)
Wicor Primary School, Portchester

DNALYRIAF

There hadn't been such a scorcher in Dnalyriaf since King George was a prince, so he was struggling to put his shorts on. Somebody arrived at his door. Hoping the mystery visitor would leave, he stayed quiet.
'Oh let him in, Henry,' said the frustrated king to his skinny butler.
Henry scurried to the door.

An old Indian man walked in, declaring to be a wizard. The king found this hard to believe as he looked like anyone else in his kingdom.
'How is it, you are India? Wizards are not Indian,' said the confused king.
The wizard, angered by the king's racist words, decided not to inform the king of the strange things that would soon affect the kingdom.

As the wizard expected, unusual things started to happen. For example, the beautiful plants got smaller until they were only bulbs. The king failed to notice the differences, so he set off to bed as usual in his four-poster bed in the twenty-seventh room of his palace, but woke from his deep sleep in a shabby villager's cottage on the hill. *This isn't me,* he thought. 'I'm going home,' he shouted.
'Pardon?' the villager's wife said.

The king and the villager discussed the many strange things that had happened and decided that they needed the help of the wizard.

'I have decided to forgive you because you have realised us Indians are just as good as you Europeans and you have to be kinder to the villagers. Your problems lie with the name of your kingdom. I now pronounce this kingdom *Fairyland!*'

Rosie Puddicombe (11)
Wicor Primary School, Portchester

THE HAND

In a derelict school at night, two young girls, one aged six called Lisa, and the other eight, called Nadine, were trying to decide whether to go into the scary old school. Their mum had told them not to go near the place, but they went into the building without looking at the sign outside: *Warning!*

As they entered, they found three corridors. Which one to choose? In the end, they chose the middle one. That was a mistake. Down came an axe, *whoosh*, a number of bats came at the girls out of nowhere. They ducked and covered their heads with their hands. All went quiet, so they carried on walking.

After a while, there was a creak and a rumble. The two girls looked at each other and whispered feebly at different times, 'Was that you?' 'No.'

Without saying anything more, they ran wildly through the corridor, in another and out another until finally stopping. Lisa giggled, thinking that it had been fun, and out of breath asked, 'Um, can we do that again?'
Instantly, Nadine shouted, 'No, no, *no!*' For a moment all was silent. Nadine froze, but Lisa was still giggling. Then she froze. There was a hand on her shoulder, a ghost-like hand. 'Aarrgghh!'

Chloe Shuttleworth (11)
Wicor Primary School, Portchester

A DAY IN THE LIFE OF AIMEE FLO

Erin was now 15, so she would stay with the adults rather than go on great adventures with Aimee, Nicky and Marianne. Everyone still remembered the time when something magic pushed the boat along.

Aimee decided to take a diary to write down what had happened, so that for years to come she could read back what had happened.
'Let's set off now, to our island!' shouted Nicky.
'We should think of a name for our island,' said Marianne.
If only Erin was here, thought Aimee.

Once again, they sailed off to the island, which they had decided to call 'Magic Island', and camped there for the night. They stayed up all night wondering what had pushed the boat, when they decided to go to bed.

When dawn rose, Aimee woke with a start. She leapt out of bed, only to find that the island was *moving!* She woke Nicky and Marianne up as fast as she could and told them that they were moving. They grabbed as much stuff as they could fit into their hands and lowered themselves into the boat and were off! Or that's what they thought.

'Oh no!' cried Nicky. 'We're still tied up to the island!'
They wrenched the rope away from the land and rowed as fast as they could. Suddenly, Erin appeared from nowhere to save them, but they could no longer see land. Aimee never got a chance to write in her diary - or did she?

Aimee White (11)
Wicor Primary School, Portchester

A DAY IN THE LIFE OF EMMA BUNTON

Emma had a busy day ahead of her and couldn't afford to be late - that was when things started to go wrong. Her alarm clock didn't work, she burnt her toast, ran out of milk and the limo was late picking her up.

Her first appointment was with her singing tutor, Miranda Tuneful. Things continued to get worse and she couldn't get in tune. Miranda was losing her patience, making Emma even more nervous. After a jumpy half hour, Emma finally managed to get in tune and Miranda calmed down.

Singing lesson over, Emma hurried along to the restaurant where she was meeting her friend for lunch. She suddenly looked at her watch - things weren't getting any better. She was late for her next appointment at the recording studio.

As she hurried down the stairs, she heard an almighty bang, then smoke coming out of the recording studio. When she got there, she saw Mike Record (the producer) and the crew on the floor. She rang for the ambulances. She was really glad she was late.

At six o'clock, she made her way home and got in a nice, warm bath. She suddenly remembered the party and leapt out of the bath. She spent ages putting on her make-up and deciding what to wear, before ringing the limo service.

Everyone famous was at the party, and Emma, had a brilliant time, even though she spilt fruit punch down her new dress

Lauren Carter (11)
Wicor Primary School, Portchester

A DAY IN THE LIFE OF A RABBIT

Once upon a time in the back garden of a very rich family, there lived a tame rabbit in a nice, big, comfy cage, cleaned out almost every day, with all the food and drink. Until one day, the owners came out of the house, leaving the rabbit thinking it was feeding time. But when they got nearer, they were carrying a box. They opened the hutch and out hopped another rabbit. As this happened, the new rabbit stampeded towards the food bowl, gobbled that up, then washed it down with some water.

This was a nightmare to the other rabbit, so he had to do something, or he would be stuck with him for the rest of his life. So they had a fight. In the end, the other rabbit won and the new rabbit lost. After that, they made friends.

Claire Huckle (10)
Wicor Primary School, Portchester

A GHOSTLY HAUNT

It was the night of Hallowe'en. Twelve-year-old Josh Samuels had just finished his trick or treating and was on his way to a deserted castle where he would meet his friends and eat his sweets. Josh was a tall, skinny boy who didn't believe in superstition or anything like it.

Josh slowly approached the castle and saw a gleaming light inside and without any doubt, went in. Once he was inside, he had a look around but no one was there; the only thing he noticed was two lit candles. He went over to the stairs and looked up. 'Is anyone there?' Josh shouted, but there was no reply. Josh then started to hear some creaks coming from upstairs, so he started to walk up the stairs.
'Sam, Alan, Mike, is that you?' asked Josh, but still no reply. Josh then saw some shadows going from room to room and began to hear some *'Whooos'*. He began to shake and slowly walked down the stairs backwards.
'Sam, if that's you, could you stop?' Josh said.

The door then began to creak open, Josh becoming even more scared.
'Oh, hi Josh,' Sam said.
'Hi,' replied Josh.
Josh decided not to tell his friends about the sounds he heard, so they all sat down and ate their sweets.

An hour later, they all had finished their sweets and so they began to chat. But then, out of the shadows came an icy hand which grabbed Josh's shoulder . . .

Matthew Longley (11)
Wicor Primary School, Portchester

DOLPHIN'S HELP

Last year on my birthday, I went to America with my family. It was a great day. We arrived at our hotel in Florida. We quickly unpacked our suitcases so we could go straight to the beach, right in front of the hotel. I ran down to the bottom of the beach to play in the sea, then I suddenly decided to make a sandcastle.

A dolphin had appeared from nowhere. The dolphin took me to a cave with lots of gold, diamonds and jewellery. I was surprised how much treasure there was, and I wondered where it had come from. I went back within an hour and took some of the treasure and put it safely into my bag, whilst my parents were asleep.

The little trip was the best thing I had dreamed of and will never be forgotten about for the rest of my life. I checked my bag, the treasure was not there . . . ?

Monica Rudd (8)
Windlesham School, Brighton

A DAY IN THE LIFE OF A COIN

It was a cold day today. I was downstairs in someone's trouser pocket.

This morning I had been to the baker's. Prudence exchanged me for some buns. I was in the till for a little while when I heard the bell jangle again, somebody came into the shop, they bought some buns too, so I knew the buns in this baker's were very popular. I was given to the man as change and he put me in his pocket.

I was just having a nap for I was already exhausted by the day's goings on, when suddenly I was pinched. I'd been the victim of a pickpocket! I was taken into the woods into the deepest part of the woods, into a cabin all covered with moss - the pickpocket's den.

It was dark in the den. The only light was a small candle. The man soon forgot about me and I was left in his pocket with his plan and a few other coins.

He soon went out to town, pickpocketing again, with me in his pocket He took out the plan with me lying on top of it - *flutter, flutter, bang!* Ow! I was lying on the pavement head first, ouch!

Just like that a little girl wearing a school dress skipped up to me and put me in her dress pocket. I was taken to the baker's but this time to buy a gingerbread man. *Ding-a-ling* the bell went again. There, standing right by he till, was guess who? Prudence! I was given to her as change. Ah, back home at last.

Jemima Poffley (8)
Windlesham School, Brighton

CHICKEN SAVES THE DAY

Once upon a time there was a chicken who lived on a farm. One night a dragon came and stamped on houses. The chicken saw this and went to kill it. He got a big hammer and a shield and went to fight it.

The dragon was fierce and could breathe fire. 'Yaaaah! I'm going to kill you.'
The dragon blew fire and the chicken got a burnt bottom.
'Yawwwwch,' cried the chicken. He hit the dragon on the head and the dragon got a bump on his head, a big one. The chicken had saved the day.

Rusteen Ordoubadian (8)
Windlesham School, Brighton

THE SILLY DINOSAURS

Once upon a time there were two dinosaurs called Rex and Velocirapter. They lived in the dinosaur age and they were good friends.

Rex felt hungry so he killed a different dinosaur. Then Velocirapter started to eat.
Rex said, 'I found this food!'
Velocirapter started to argue with Rex.

As they were fighting, a triceratops stole their food. Rex and Velocirapter had realised how silly they had been and apologised to each other.

Alexander Baboulene (8)
Windlesham School, Brighton

THE HAUNTED HOUSE

One morning, Mario woke up. The postman arrived with a letter. The letter said his aunt had left him a house in her will. Mario was excited. He had been living in his friend's garden shed for 5 years.

Mario decided to visit the house. He packed his bag and off he went. When he arrived he took out the key. The door creaked open. There were cobwebs hanging, the furniture was very old.

When it was night-time there were funny noises. Mario said, 'Who's there?'
The ghost said, 'How dare you come to this house!'
The next morning Mario packed his bags and sold the house!

Henry Henley (8)
Windlesham School, Brighton

THE MYSTERY OF THE SCIENTIST

Once, ten years ago, there was a mad scientist called Malcolm. He was building a time machine and it blew up. When he was buried, he came back alive.

There were three children called David, Alex and Abs. David was 8 years old and was very lively and very tall for his age. David was very good at school. He liked football, cricket, rugby and basketball. Alex was 10 years old. He was very small for his age. Alex never paid attention at school. Alex liked rugby, football, PlayStation games and pizza. He disliked cabbage! Abs was 7 years old. He liked football, cricket and nature.

Malcolm came back to haunt the headmaster, his brother, because he gave him the wrong parts for the time machine. While Malcolm and the headmaster were talking, the children caught Malcolm with a ghost catcher and put him back in his grave. After that, the headmaster regretting giving Malcolm the wrong parts for the time machine.

Gabriel Panayiotou (8)
Windlesham School, Brighton

THE THIRSTY KANGAROO

It was dry, hot and red. A thirsty kangaroo was looking for the waterhole. He met a noisy, laughing kookaburra and he asked if he knew where the waterhole was. The kookaburra told him to follow the wombat trail.

They found a fat, slow wombat. The three found the waterhole but it was dry! The kangaroo told the wombat to dig deep down.

After a long time, the wombat said, 'I see water!'
They were all saved.

Megan Larner (8)
Windlesham School, Brighton

THE MAN

It is early morning. I stand by the window waiting for that man with the big bag. Here he comes again. He steps up towards our door. I shout and shout but he does not seem to hear. I shout louder and louder but he still keeps coming towards our door.

I dash down the hall and Charlie, the rough boy, whacks me on the bottom. Daisy, the sweet girl, shouts my name. I get to the front door, but too late. The man with the bag pushes those things through the hole in the door and they land on my head. Daisy and Charlie laugh.

I'm fed up! I'm going for a sniff round the dishwasher, then I'm going to bury my bone.

Daisy Milner (8)
Windlesham School, Brighton

THE GHOST TRAIN

On a normal bank holiday Monday, a girl called Mary went to the funfair. She went on the helter-skelter, funhouse, roller coaster, a really big slide and the bumper cars. The only thing she had not been on was the ghost train. As Mary made her way up to the ghost train, someone screamed.

'Help! That ghost train is haunted!' The lady then said to Mary, 'Come on, I'll show you!' The lady was in a right panic.

'All right, all right, keep your hair on!' said Mary.

As she was walking with the lady, she heard a click. Somebody had dropped a charm bracelet. 'Wow, I'm keeping this!' said Mary.

Mary went on the ghost train. She saw a skeleton, spiders, ghosts and a witch. Suddenly she heard a clanking noise and an eerie scream. The hairs on Mary's neck stood on end. *'Get me out of here!'* Mary screamed. Suddenly the ghost train came out into the sunlight, the ride was over.

'Phew!' said Mary. 'Now I know what the lady meant by a haunted ghost train.'

Jessica Price (8)
Windlesham School, Brighton

THE TWO TINY FAIRIES

There were two fairies, one called Buttercup and one called Rose. They lived in a garden and used flowers as their homes. At night they would fly into houses and sprinkle glittery fairy dust over the children. When the children woke up the next day they had magical powers. Sometimes the children were able to do hard sums easily and sometimes they could clean their rooms in a flash.

One night a child woke up when the fairies were sprinkling the fairy dust and it stopped all the magic from working. The fairies were very sad as they could not stay anymore. Once they had been seen, they had to go back to their magic castle in the clouds.

Romina Duplain (8)
Windlesham School, Brighton

TWO SIDES TO EVERY STORY

Chapter 1

'Look at the sea, it's so beautiful, it matches your eyes,' Ken whispered over the seagulls and the competing waves, each trying to rise higher and higher. 'I love you so much Sabrina.' Ken looked deeply into her eyes as he carried on. 'Don't ever leave me.' His hand reached up to touch her face, tracing her perfectly curved cheekbones, staring intently into her eyes, his face showing more than he could ever explain to her.

'I wouldn't dream of it,' Sabrina answered as she leaned in to give Ken a gentle kiss. Suddenly she had the urge to carry on, to make it something better. He did it for her; she could feel his hands working down from her face towards her waist. His lips tasted of strawberries, pressing down on her own. She could feel the passion of the kiss as his hands wrapped themselves around her back.

It was Sabrina's 17th birthday. Ken went with her on a long walk on the beach. They had walked for hours, hand in hand, telling each other of their hopes and dreams. They opened up to each other in a way they had never done before. Even though they had only been together a couple of weeks, they both felt that they had been together for years. Now they were sitting at the edge of the beach, their toes in the water, watching the Californian sun drowning in the calm water.

As they slowly parted, Ken realised that he hadn't yet given her her birthday present. He reached into their picnic basket and rooted round a little until he found it. 'Here's your present, I hope you like it!'
'I thought that kiss was my present!' she joked as she took the present. She gently poked her finger through a hole in the wrapping paper. As she slid it sideways she tried to figure out what it could be. As she withdrew her finger, she reached up with her other hand and slid off the wrapping paper. It was a little red box. She recognised it as a jewellery box from a famous jeweller called Andrew Cox. As she turned it over, she slid in her long, painted fingernail; she pulled upwards, lifting up the lid. She withdrew her finger in shock . . .

Samantha Hickey (11)
Velmead Junior School, Fleet

THE LOST CAT

One night a little girl called Sophie had left the kitchen window open and the family cat called Fuzzy climbed out of the window. The morning after, when Sophie called Fuzzy for breakfast, Sophie saw that she was not in her bed. Sophie realised that she might have climbed out of the window and gone for good.

All of the family had written letters to nearly all of the street asking them that if they were to see a brown and white tabby could they please call the number on the note. It had been about a week but they had not heard from anyone.

'Where could our little Fuzzy have got to?' asked Liz, Sophie's mum.
'There's the phone ringing. Someone might have found her.'
'No luck. She has gone for good,' cried Sophie.
The family had split up. Josh, Sophie's dad, went with James, Sophie's brother, and Sophie and Liz went together to look for Fuzzy.

That night, James heard a '*miaow, miaow*' but it was only their other cat, Teacup. Teacup came in and sat down on his bed.
'What was that?' asked Sophie, trembling.
'It's only the thunder and lightning,' said James, trying to get his sister to calm down. 'What's that? I can hear Teacup miaowing.'
'Let's go and see,' said Sophie.
They both saw some eyes at the cat flap.
'Those are cat's eyes,' said James and Sophie.
They went to the cat flap and bent down.
'It's Fuzzy, she's come back,' shouted Sophie.

She had woken her mum and dad up, so the parents went downstairs.
Liz said, 'What are you shouting for?'
'Fuzzy's back!' the children shouted.
'Fuzzy's back,' the parents said.
'Let's feed her,' said Sophie.

That's the end. They found their lost cat, Fuzzy, so now Sophie knows not to leave the window open.

Kelly Hanshew (10)
Velmead Junior School, Fleet

ELIZABETH'S EAGLE

There once lived a boy called Andy who was eight years old and lived with his mum and dad. They were going to move house soon. Andy wasn't very excited.

'Mum,' he asked one day, 'do we have to move?'
'Why, yes dear,' answered his mother. 'Why do you ask?'
'Because I will miss our neighbours and friends,' continued Andy. 'I'll be bored.'
'There'll be lots of things to do, trust me,' said Mum. 'You never know who you might meet.'
'Cheer up,' said Dad when he came home from work, 'there'll be lots of things to do, trust me.'
Why is everybody saying the same thing? he thought to himself.

Finally the day came and Andy was looking out of the window. 'I don't want to move house!' he cried as if somebody had hurt him, and huge tears were rolling down his face. 'I'll be lonely and have nobody to play with!' With tears still streaming down his face, he wiped his eyes with his T-shirt.
Just then Mum called, 'Andy, we're ready to go!'
'Just coming,' said Andy drearily as if somebody had told him bad news. When he got outside, he watched the removal lorry leave and then got into Dad's car.

When they arrived at their new home, they got out of the car. While Dad and the driver of the lorry were unpacking, Mum whispered something to Andy.
'Why don't you go inside and explore?' she said. 'Here's a torch, go and look round.'
'Okay Mum,' said Andy unhappily, drooping like a gorilla as he walked along.

When he reached the top of the stairs he saw a rope ladder hanging down. He struggled up the ladder to find the attic. It was old, dusty and completely empty and seemed a bit damp as well. Suddenly there was a noise that sounded like the wind whistling, but Andy wasn't afraid. Then he caught sight of something in the corner in the torch light - it was a lamp. Although it was dusty-looking, it still shone. Andy felt like somebody was urging him to rub the lamp. As he crept cautiously towards the glittering object like a tiger ready to pounce, he reached out and rubbed it. He felt as if something was moving, alive inside.

'Who's there?' he called fearlessly as he rubbed the lamp again. Then a ghost appeared. It stood there as white as snow but Andy could make out the shape of a girl's face. 'W-w-who are you?' murmured Andy nervously under his breath. 'Why are you here?'
'Hello,' said the ghost. 'I'm Elizabeth and . . .' She explained that she had come back for her precious eagle jewel and that she used to live in the house long ago and couldn't rest until it was found.
'I'll help you find it!' cried Andy in delight. At least he had something to do. 'I'd be honoured. Where shall we look?'
'Why, here, thank you!' smiled Elizabeth beaming with joy.
Andy smiled back.

They looked for it for a long time until Andy said, 'Why don't we call my friend, Jake, round to help? He lives not far away.'
'Good idea,' said the ghost.

When Jake arrived, Andy led him up to the attic. He rubbed the lamp and out popped the ghost. When they had introduced each other they all started looking.

Eventually, Jake trod on a loose floorboard and it bounced back on him. 'Ouch!' he cried. 'What was that?'
Andy called to the others, 'Look under here, there is a shiny chest, that is what made you bounce backwards.'
'Let's see,' said Jake.
'Let me see too,' cried Elizabeth, wanting to know what all the commotion was about.
'Come on, let's open it then,' said Andy. Just as he put his hand out to touch it, black stifling smoke came whooshing out. The children jerked back as two hot, hairy hands appeared and then a daring dotty dragon became visible.
'*Roar!*' he snarled, screwing up his face. 'You can only open this chest if you can find the key and you'll never be able to do that, will you?' He growled a horrible laugh.
'Oh, that's what you think, is it?' retorted Andy, revealing a bad-tempered look on his face.

They looked behind doors, underneath furniture, but soon they found a piece of paper with a riddle on it. It said:

'The time never stands still
The time goes forwards not backwards,
You need a key to wind me up
Take it and you will see
Something that happens magically'.

'It must be a riddle to help us!' cried Andy. 'Well, time is represented by a clock!'

'Of course!' said Elizabeth.

'Yes, but what kind of clock?' asked Jake.

'One that has a key to wind it up.'

Just then, Mum called. 'Boys, dinner is ready.'

'Okay, coming!' shouted Andy.

As they passed the lounge they saw Dad hanging up something . . . it was a cuckoo clock.

'Hey, the cuckoo clock has a key to wind it up, doesn't it?' cried Andy. They ran into the lounge.

'Dad, is there a key to that clock?' asked Andy hopefully.

'Why yes, here it is,' said Dad.

'Can we borrow it?' asked Jake excitedly.

The boys quickly returned to the attic to find Elizabeth sleeping.

'Elizabeth, Elizabeth!' shouted the boys. 'We've got a key, let's see if it fits.'

The boys showed her the key and then they lifted up the floorboard again and the dragon appeared. The dragon let them try out the key and it opened the chest and there it was, the eagle jewel - glowing brightly.

Elizabeth lurched towards the jewel and grasped it tightly in her hands and slowly faded away, calling out to the boys, 'Thank you, thank you.' The dragon vanished in a puff of black smoke and the boys were left on their own.

'I think I am going to like my new house,' announced Andy with a smile.

Juliette Colver (8)
Velmead Junior School, Fleet

THE RUNAWAY

Once upon a time there was a little girl called Stella with brown hair and blue eyes. She lived in a cottage in the middle of a forest with her mum and her dad. One day, when Stella and her mum were arguing, Stella had thought she had a good idea of running away. She was only 5 so she did not know what it would be like to be homeless. She went into her bedroom and started to pack.

The very next day she left home. She left a little note saying, 'I am going to see my friend on the other side of the world. Bye', in very messy writing.
'She does not know where she is going and who knows what dangers lie ahead of her?' screeched her mum when she found the note.

'Where am I?' Stella mumbled to herself as she was sitting among some thorns.

As night fell, Stella's mum and dad became terrified so they started to make missing posters because they could not find her anywhere.

When the sun rose and morning came, Stella began to search for a place to stay and something to eat and drink. Something caught Stella's eyes, it was a train station with a café, but she could not buy anything because she didn't have any money. Luckily a train came past so she quickly got on and pretended to be with someone. She would not have to pay but that person would and she could take the tickets from the people and go and sit by herself. She did that and it all went according to plan. She sat down by herself.

Stella looked at the person opposite who was staring out of the window. She seemed to recognise her. It was her friend who she was going to see.
'Holly,' said Stella, who was still rather surprised.
'Stella,' Holly said in amazement.
'I was just coming to see you.'
'Why?'
'Because I ran away from home.'
'Oh, right. Why?'
'Me and my mum were arguing so I ran away.'

'Where did you sleep last night?'
'In a pile of rubbish.'
'That is awful, you will have to sleep at my house.'

When they got to Holly's house, Stella was allowed to ring her mum so she could come and pick her up. After a while Stella's mum came and picked her up and took her home. Stella's mum gave her loads of hugs and kisses and said she was sorry.

After a while, Holly's family moved house and came to live down Stella's road. They could now play together any day or any time. The following day they all went down to the beach to find some crabs and nice shells.

Ashlie Martin (10)
Velmead Junior School, Fleet

THE BURIED KEY

'One of the maize plants isn't doing very well, Dad,' I said, 'the one nearest the fence.'

'I know,' my dad said, sighing.

My family owned a farm by the sea. I lived with my mum, my dad and my Labrador, Joe. I also had a friend called Andrew who visited us often.

Ding-dong! Ding-dong!

'Andrew's here!' called my mum.

'OK!' I replied. 'Hi Andrew, you all right?'

Andrew had blondish hair, brown eyes and an oval face and he wasn't as tall as me.

'Yes,' Andrew replied, 'let's go and have a look at that odd maize plant.'

'OK, let's go!' I said. 'Race you.'

I said goodbye to my mum and dad and rushed after Andrew.

Suddenly, Joe, my Labrador, darted as fast as he could after us.

When we got there, Andrew said, 'If the plant is diseased, let's dig it up.'

'Good idea,' I agreed. 'I'm sure that my parents will be pleased.'

'*Woof!*' barked Joe.

'Let's get a spade from the shed,' I said.

So Andrew went to get the spade. When he came back we dug and dug around the roots of the plant. I started to pull at the plant and at last I got it out. At the end of the roots was a key, a bright silver key, that glistened in the sunlight. Andrew and I stared at each other in astonishment. As I fixed my eyes on it, I found writing. It said '*2004*'.

Suddenly, out of the blue, appeared a ghost who looked pretty much like a Roman soldier.

'Who are you?' said Andrew and I in shock and surprise.

'I am a Roman ghost,' replied the figure, 'I have come to tell you about the key. The key belongs to Janus, our god.'

'Didn't we learn about Janus at school?' enquired Andrew.

'Yes, I think we did,' I replied, somewhat perplexed.

'*Woof!*' barked Joe.

'Anyway,' interrupted the ghost, 'you need to give it back to him.'

'But how? Where do we find him?' questioned Andrew.
'Go down to the beach and see,' persuaded the soldier again.
'*Woof, woof,*' whimpered Joe. It sounded like he was scared.
'OK . . . let's go.' To be honest with you, I felt a little frightened too.
Just then the figure said, 'Goodbye,' in a ghost-like voice and faded.
'Well, you heard what he said, come on!' Andrew yelled.
'Er . . . yes,' I whispered, petrified.

Joe whimpered a small 'woof' again miserably, but still followed and I felt the same way. Joe plodded and I slouched as we followed Andrew down to the beach. The bright blue sky above was dotted with white, fluffy clouds.

As we came to the edge of the sea something started to appear. It was a small ghost ship. We all looked in amazement. My heart pounded like thunder. The key sent an electric shock through me and made me shiver We knew what we had to do.

'All aboard!' bellowed Andrew.
Joe made a tiny whimper.
'O-OK,' I stammered. Carrying Joe with me I stepped onto the small ship. Andrew pushed us into the sea. He leapt aboard.
'I've got wet feet now,' Andrew grumbled.
I gave a modest snigger.
'*Woof!*' yapped Joe, happily.
That made me happier, but Andrew, on the other hand, said, 'What's so funny?'
'Nothing,' I said, as though nothing had happened.
Just then, I noticed Joe pointing up with his paw. I felt that it wasn't good news. I slowly manoeuvred my head to look at the blue sky.
'Oh no, it's . . . it's!' I began.
'Mmmist!' finished Andrew.
'*Hoowwwl!*' Joe howled.
Suddenly, I heard something galloping in our direction. There, in the sky, were three Roman horses and carts.
'I know where they have come from,' Andrew said proudly. 'Janus sent them to guide us.'
'He must have heard Joe's howl,' I exclaimed.

So, (as Andrew said), we followed the horses and soon after, the impenetrable mist cleared. Behind the mist an island appeared. I noticed that it was in the shape of a Roman soldier. When I saw this I felt cold sweat dropping down my spine.

When we had stepped off the *ghost* ship we stared back at it, but it had vanished. There was only one word I could say about this, *weird!* I gazed down at Joe and so did Andrew.
'Do you think he's picked up an odd smell?' asked Andrew.
But before I could answer Joe was walking to an opening in the cliffs.
'A secret entrance or something,' said Andrew feeling rather puzzled, 'yes, I think it *is* a secret entrance.'
'Maybe we'll meet Janus in there,' I remarked. 'We'd better catch up with Joe otherwise we'll lose him.'
'Have you got the key?' said Andrew.
'Yes, I'll put it in my pocket,' I replied.

As we went in the mysterious cave I saw candles in small baskets. I took two and gave one to Andrew. We started to worry as Joe was out of sight, but Andrew and I felt he was out of harm's way. The cave was as dark as night. Only the candles led the way. Then the corridor split into two.
'What now?' I said.
'Well, don't look at me,' Andrew snapped.

When we thought we might as well turn back, there was a deafening *yap,* which came from the right passage, so that's the way we went. A few minutes later, Andrew and I were standing in what looked like a lounge. I knew where we were. *We were in the Kingdom of Janus.* There was a blazing fire, a wooden bookshelf and pictures of Romans, but best of all was in the centre of the room, Janus *himself.* I can't really describe him very well because he looked so odd. He was quite small, wore funny clothes and the weirdest thing was that he had two faces!

When I stared at Janus more, I realised that he was not alone. Out jumped Joe.
'Joe!' I cried, 'I've been looking everywhere for you.'
'Welcome children to the land of the Roman gods,' Janus said boldly.
'Yes Sir, thank you Sir,' Andrew responded.

'I believe you have come to give me something,' stated Janus, twiddling his fingers.

'Yes,' I replied, 'I think you mislaid a key. The key to 2004.'

At this moment Joe lay down and went very quiet.

'Let me see,' requested the two-headed god.

'I'll just get it out of my pocket,' I said.

When I had it in my hand I gave it to Janus.

'Well, well, you are very nice children,' he exclaimed.

'Excuse me,' interrupted Andrew. 'Could I just ask you a question and then I think we should be getting back. What do you need the key for?'

'*Woof!*' barked Joe.

'Well . . . ' said Janus, 'I need to key so I can open the door to the Year 2004. If I don't, then all the people will have to go to the after world.'

'Sorry to interrupt, but please can we go home now?' I pleaded.

'Ah yes,' Janus declared, 'but before you go I would like to give you something each.'

He reached under his chair and pulled out a small bag. He put his hand inside and pulled out two ornaments of a Roman soldier. He also pulled out a Roman soldier toy. I think it was made out of cloth. 'There you go my friends,' he said. 'I will come and wave you off.'

So off we went. Joe was a bit tired so I carried him. When we were outside, Janus whispered to me, 'I know your friend means a lot to you and you will always be friends. Bye for now.'

When I looked at the shore the ghost ship was appearing again. Andrew, Joe and I climbed into the ship and Janus pushed us off and waved. We waved back. What an adventure it had been.

A few hours later it was bedtime. Andrew was having a sleepover and Joe sat in his warm basket. On my shelf were the gifts that Janus had given us. Andrew and Joe were fast asleep, but I sat up awake. I was thinking about what Janus had said to me about Andrew. He was right about Andrew meaning a lot to me. I would be friends with Andrew forever and ever.

Sarah-Jane Colver (8)
Velmead Junior School, Fleet

A Day In The Life Of My Dad!

Right, imagine yourself a man who seems to only ever care about his business, marketing. (Don't ask me, I don't have a clue what it is, I keep asking my dad what it is, but I don't understand it when he tells me!) Right, back to the subject. This man who you are imagining yourself to be has quite scruffy handwriting but to himself it's readable and quite neat. He knows everything about computers. He has two kids, James who's 13 and Abby who's 10. He also has a wife called Claire who's a nurse, and last and most important of all, his name is Phil (Philip).

In your imagination, you have now become Phil. You have brown hair - not much of it though! And you wear glasses when you're tired. This particular day you're working at home - you usually work at Thame near Oxford or are abroad at some meeting or other. You're working at home so your kids can get in because your wife's at work. Because you're working at home, you have a lie-in. 7.30! That's not a lie-in! You get up to go to the loo, come out and today you have to make your children's breakfast because your wife's busy making the beds and has to go to work very soon. You get out the toaster, frying pan and an egg. You fry the egg and give them egg on toast. You then go upstairs and switch on your laptop and check if you've received any new e-mails throughout the duration of your sleep. You've received 55. You reply to them all.

You then get dressed into normal clothes, not a suit, and return to your laptop. You put your headphones on which you can call and talk to people with, you lift up the phone off the hook in front of you and dial a number to join a two hour conference call. You've finished the conference and it's now time for lunch.

You make a ham, cheese, lettuce and tomato sandwich, put it on a plate with a packet of cheese and onion crisps, you then go to the fridge and get a can of Coke out. You then go back upstairs to your office and eat it.

After you've finished your lunch, you then ring up your work colleagues and discuss about one of the projects you're doing and discuss boring stuff like data. It's now 12.30, you have an hour long meeting in Guilford, you estimate that it takes roughly about 20 minutes to get there, so you should be home at about 2ish. As you're running a bit late, you run down the stairs, out the front door and over to your Mercedes-Benz, you press the unlock button and pull the back door open. You then throw your bag on the back seats, close the back door and open the front one. You sit down quickly on your lovely leather seat and put the key in the ignition. You put your seat belt on and then start driving. Then there's a beeping noise - you've forgotten to release your handbrake. You pull it, then start driving to Guilford.

You get there and you discuss boring things about starting a new project. It goes on for longer than you think because you're so 'polite'. You don't excuse the meeting so you can be home for your children - uh! Your son comes in at 3.00 and your daughter comes in at 3.30. Luckily you just get in 2 minutes before your son, James. You let James in, he comes upstairs and starts doing his art homework. You start working again.

Half an hour later, there's another ring at the doorbell. You answer it, this time it's your daughter, Abby. You give her a hug and say, 'Did you have a nice day at school?'
I (Abby) usually reply yes or no and then go in to the lounge and watch TV - if it's not a particularly nice day!

You then go straight back to work and then a quarter of an hour later, guess who's ringing on the doorbell? You wife, Claire, but this time, James answers the door.
Claire shouts to you, 'Hello-o.'
You then answer back, 'Hi.' You then hear distant talking from where Claire is talking to Abby (me).

You carry on your so-far boring day. I don't actually know what you do next, you probably just sit at your computer and do some more work. Well, anyway, Claire sends me up to tell you that dinner is ready. You hear me come up I tell you.
You reply, 'Okay, I'll be down in a minute.' You save your work and come down the stairs, into the kitchen and then into the conservatory where the table and chairs are and where three people are waiting for you to come and sit down and eat. You eat your dinner; pork chops,

beans, carrots and mash potato. You go back upstairs and close the computer down. You've finished work, eventually!

You go back downstairs and switch on the widescreen TV and start watching. It's now time for me to go to bed. I get into bed and call you and Claire. You give me a kiss goodnight, you then go back downstairs and make yourself a coffee and a cup of tea each for Claire and James. You go into the lounge where they are and give them their teas and sit down with them and drink your coffee. An hour later, it's time for James to go to bed. You and Claire say goodnight, then you watch even more TV!

Eventually, an hour and a half later, it's time for you and Claire to go to bed. Claire starts reading her fifth Harry Potter book and you start reading your third Lord Of The Rings book. You read for about half an hour and then you and Claire decide to go to sleep. You then fall asleep!

So now you know what a day feels like of being . . . *my dad!*

Abby Gowing (10)
Velmead Junior School, Fleet